PUFFIN BOOKS

Something Invisible

Siobhán Parkinson is one of Ireland's leading authors for children and teenagers, and she has won numerous awards for her writing. Her books have been translated into many languages, from Danish to Thai – even ones where they translate your name as well as your book, so somewhere in Central Europe are books by a person called Šivena Parkinsona.

She is joint editor of *Bookbird*, an international journal on children's literature, and when she is not writing stories or pretending to be Šivena Parkinsona, she visits schools and works with children on their writing projects. Siobhán lives in Dublin with her husband and grown-up son.

Puffin Books by Siobhán Parkinson

SECOND FIDDLE
SOMETHING INVISIBLE

Something Invisible

SIOBHÁN PARKINSON

PUFFIN

PUFFIN BOOKS

Published by the Penguin Group
Penguin Books Ltd, 80 Strand, London WC2R ORL, England
Penguin Group (USA) Inc., 375 Hudson Street, New York, New York 10014, USA
Penguin Group (Canada), 90 Eglinton Avenue East, Suite 700, Toronto, Ontario, Canada M4P 2Y3
(a division of Pearson Penguin Canada Inc.)
Penguin Ireland, 25 St Stephen's Green, Dublin 2, Ireland (a division of Penguin Books Ltd)
Penguin Group (Australia), 250 Camberwell Road, Camberwell, Victoria 3124, Australia
(a division of Pearson Australia Group Pty Ltd)
Penguin Books India Pvt Ltd, 11 Community Centre, Panchsheel Park, New Delhi – 110 017, India
Penguin Group (NZ), cnr Airborne and Rosedale Roads, Albany, Auckland 1310, New Zealand
(a division of Pearson New Zealand Ltd)
Penguin Books (South Africa) (Pty) Ltd, 24 Sturdee Avenue, Rosebank, Johannesburg 2196, South Africa

Penguin Books Ltd, Registered Offices: 80 Strand, London WC2R ORL, England

www.penguin.com

First published 2006
1

Copyright © Siobhán Parkinson, 2006
All rights reserved

The moral right of the author has been asserted

Set in Baskerville MT by Palimpsest Book Production Limited, Polmont, Stirlingshire
Made and printed in England by Clays Ltd, St Ives plc

British Library Cataloguing in Publication Data
A CIP catalogue record for this book is available from the British Library

ISBN-13: 978-0-141-31883-7
ISBN-10: 0-141-31883-X

*To Oisín, my beloved nephew and godson,
a smashing reader and a super critic*

The Daisy follows soft the Sun –
And when his golden walk is done –
Sits shyly at his feet.
He – waking – finds the flower there –
Wherefore – Marauder – art thou here?
Because, Sir, love is sweet!

Emily Dickinson

1

Nobody ever blamed Jake for what happened.

2

Except himself.

3

But let's go back to the beginning.

4

There was a girl at the bus stop. She looked about Jake's age, or maybe a bit older. He didn't usually notice girls much, except to make a mental note to avoid them. That was because he found they generally acted superior, which unsettled him. But he noticed this one because she was so thin. Not undernourished thin. More sort of greyhound thin. Her long, wispy hair was pale brown or dark blonde, no colour really; that made her even more greyhoundish.

She had two of those very green shopping bags, the ones that last forever, one dragging her right arm down and one on the ground, between her feet. Two younger children who were playing on the pavement behind seemed to be vaguely attached to her. They never looked at her, nor she at them; nor did they speak to each other. But somehow Jake knew they were together. Something invisible linked them.

The bag at her feet had a tube of aluminium

7

foil in it, the extra-big kind, for turkeys, which was too long to balance properly among the rest of the shopping. Jake noticed that she tipped at it with her knee, to keep it from falling over.

She was waiting for the same bus as he was, but when it came it was full to bursting, and the driver only allowed two people on board, Jake and an old lady on an aluminium stick that had three little legs with rubber feet. The girl and the younger children pressed forward and looked hopeful, but the driver shook his head and pointed over his shoulder, to indicate that there was another bus coming soon.

Jake dithered for a moment. He ought to let the girl on instead of him – not because she was a girl, but because of all the shopping – only there wouldn't be room for the children too, and they would only get in the way of the woman on the funny stick, trip her up, even. She didn't look as if she could cope with small children getting tangled in her stick.

So in the end he got on the bus and squirmed his way into a gap between two tall people. He didn't have much space, but at least he could see out of the window. He watched as the thin girl transferred the bag with the long tube of foil in it to her hand, and put the other bag, which looked lumpy and heavier, at her feet instead. She put her chin to the top of the foil carton to steady it and shuffled her feet to make space for the other bag between them. Then Jake's bus drifted away from the bus stop and he lost sight of her.

5

He swam up out of a dream in the night and thought, someone should tell her about the other kind of aluminium foil you can get. It comes in a shorter roll, like cling film, which makes it easier to manage in your shopping bag. Though she might be going to cook a turkey, of course, in which case maybe she needed the longer foil. He didn't know much about cooking.

6

His mother woke him in the morning, as she always did, by chucking his curtains open. He flung his arm over his eyes to shut out the painful sunlight. She drew the top sheet over his head and said, 'OK, you can take your arm away now.' Under the sheet, he moved his arm gingerly away from his face and opened his eyes. His eyelashes brushed the fabric of the sheet, which filtered the light. The smell of washing powder and fabric conditioner mingled in his nostrils with his own slight whiff. Slowly, he slid the sheet down and faced the daylight.

His mother was standing at an angle, looking out of the window, but partly turned towards the room, and him. Her body was outlined against the light. She'd got awfully fat lately, heavy and slow, but her hair was the same as ever, wild and rich and bright. He liked looking at her, blurred against the sunshine. It made her seem more herself. He couldn't explain it, but it made him want to touch her, to put out a hand and stroke her arm or finger her hair.

He wouldn't, though. That'd be soppy.

'Come on, Jake, breakfast time,' she said, turning towards him. She sounded tired. 'Hot or cold milk on your cornflakes?'

'Hot,' he said. 'Thanks,' he added.

By the time he got downstairs, though, the milk was only lukewarm. There's a lot to do in the mornings. He'd read that you should brush your teeth before breakfast, for example, not after, and that took time, among other things.

'Do you think a person could have a job making up colour names?' Jake asked as he dug into the lukewarm cereal, hardly realizing he was speaking aloud.

He'd been thinking about it for a while. He often thought about things that didn't seem to occur to other people. Not that this was a job he thought he would like to have himself, because he was going to be a fish painter when he grew up, but he wondered all the same about where the paint names came from.

'Colours already have names,' his dad said. He was one of the other people who didn't seem to think about the kinds of things that Jake thought about. He was eating toast and reading the paper, in that jolly, Dad-ish, what-a-lot-of-endearing-rubbish-you-think way. 'Red, orange, yellow . . .'

Breakfast was the only meal where you were allowed to read in Jake's family, but Jake never wanted to read at the table; he preferred talking. Thinking and talking were his favourite things, next to football and fish.

'No,' said Jake. 'I mean, like on paint cards: "Applemint", "Aqua", "Sunburst", "Cinnabar".' You had to spell things out for Dad.

'Donkey,' said his dad.

'I know what you mean,' said Jake. 'A sort of greyish brown. Or brownish grey.'

'No, I mean, that's what you are.' His dad grinned stupidly. 'A donkey. Hee-haw.'

Jake ignored this, or pretended to. 'Stickleback,' he added.

'Stickleback?'

'They go blue,' Jake explained. 'The males. And red. But mostly blue.'

'People wouldn't know that,' his dad said. '*Normal* people, I mean, about sticklebacks going blue, so it wouldn't mean anything.'

'They would know it,' said Jake reasonably, 'even normal people, if they'd got our encyclopedia, the one we have at school. There's a picture of a stickleback when it goes blue. Anyway, "Cinnabar" doesn't mean anything either. Or "Aqua". Water is colourless – usually. That's how you can see the fish so clearly.'

Jake had a fish tank in his room. There were

tropical fish in it, scarlet and royal blue and zebra-striped, and rocks with fronds and pieces of coral (not real coral, as far as he knew) and grit in the bottom and a thing shaped like a sugar cane that bubbled. He liked to look at the tropical fish, from time to time, because they were pretty, but he wasn't especially interested in them – they were like slowly moving wallpaper – and he wouldn't have bothered with a fish tank himself. He was more interested in real fish. But he never let on to his dad, because the tank had been a present for his last birthday and Dad was dead proud of having bought him such a cool present.

Jake's dad tried pretty hard to be mates with him, and Jake tried to remember to appreciate that. Sometimes it was tough going.

'What makes them go blue?' his dad asked now.

'Fatherhood,' Jake said.

Jake's dad coughed. He coughed and coughed and splattered toast crumbs all over his plate. Jake ran the tap and filled a glass of water for him.

'Here,' he said. 'Drink this. Aqua, haitch-two-oh, a colourless liquid, key substance for life on earth, boiling point one hundred degrees, freezing point zero.'

He'd learnt that from the encyclopedia, the one at school with the blue stickleback picture in it. He liked encyclopedias. He usually took one down from the shelf during Reading Time on Fridays.

The girls always read storybooks. That was another reason he didn't much like girls, the way they were always reading stories. He bet they did it just to please the teachers. Teachers thought you were great if you liked reading stories. But Jake had noticed that teachers were mostly girls, or used to be, which probably explained this.

'Did you know that a litre of water weighs a kilo?' Jake said, watching as his dad drank the water.

'No,' said Dad. 'That's extraordinary. What a coincidence!'

Jake sighed. There was no point in talking to some people. They just didn't get it.

Dad stood up from the table and jerked his arms a few times, to make the tips of his shirt cuffs appear out from under the sleeves of his jacket. That meant he was getting ready to leave for work.

'Good lad,' he said, catching Jake's eye watching him.

Jake didn't know what he'd done to deserve this kindly form of address, but he nodded gravely all the same and tried to look as if he was indeed an excellent lad that any father would be proud of.

Lavender Dusk, he thought, as his dad left the room. He'd seen this weird poppy yesterday at the edge of the football pitch, not a wild one, but growing wild. If there were a paint the colour of the poppy, that's what he'd call it.

'Lavender Dusk,' he said, trying the sound of it aloud.

The front door banged.

He asked his mother what that made her think of.

'Lavender Dusk? Sounds like a lipstick,' she said unpoetically. She was often unpoetic; he'd noticed that about her, though she was supposed to be a poet.

'Oh!' said Jake, taken aback. Disappointed.

It did. That spoilt it.

7

The baby was a girl.

8

His mother hadn't got fat. She'd been having a baby.

They told him about it, of course, his parents, in the end, before the baby actually arrived. They'd meant to mention it earlier, they said, but somehow . . . They thought it was OK to end a sentence like that, just trailing off, with 'but somehow . . .' *He* wouldn't get away with it. Jake kicked the kitchen press with the side of his foot. There was a scuffed place where he always did that when he was confused or cross.

'We kept thinking,' his mother said in a high, false-sounding voice, 'he's sure to notice, and we kept waiting for you to notice, but you kept on not noticing, and then, somehow, it all seemed . . .' His mother's voice fell back to its normal pitch, and then it trailed away again.

Jake hung his head. He felt stupid. At his age, not to notice a thing like that! But then, why should he? There are other things to think about, school and football and fish and stuff. You don't go around noticing that your mother's pregnant, do you? You don't think of your mother as a reproducing female, as if she's a classroom pet or a laboratory animal. She's your mum, isn't she?

If he'd been a girl he might have noticed. If he'd been a girl, they might have told him sooner. No, he didn't feel stupid; he felt they *thought* he'd been stupid. But that seemed worse, somehow. He felt himself getting hot and confused. He gave the door of the press another furtive sidelong kick.

'We didn't want to force you to face it,' his mother was saying now, half apologetically. 'I did try to mention it a few times. I did bring the subject up once or twice. But you just didn't seem to be ready to talk about it. So we thought we'd let you come to it in your own time, Jake. Jake?' She was peering at him with an anxious expression.

Jake tried to remember her bringing the subject up, but he couldn't. He'd give her the benefit of the doubt, he thought, but he felt a bit conned all the same. He couldn't say that, of course, because then there'd be a row and he didn't want there to be a row about the baby. That'd be awful. It wasn't the baby's fault. Poor little scrap. Not that he was all that keen on babies, but you couldn't go blaming them for stuff.

So he said nothing; just shrugged. And they

laughed at him, his parents, for not noticing something so obvious. But it wasn't a mean laugh; it was a relieved laugh. It was as if they'd expected him to be upset and they were glad to see that he wasn't. Why should he be upset? That would be silly, to be upset about a little baby. So he joined in and laughed too; that way, they'd know it was OK, he was OK about it. They all laughed at Jake, with Jake, and his mum and dad stroked the baby's skin with wondering fingers.

'It's the best thing that's ever happened,' his dad said. 'Isn't it, Jake? The very best thing ever.'

'Umm,' said Jake.

'A miracle,' said his dad. 'That's what she is, a little miracle. My miracle daughter.'

'She's – eh . . .' But Jake couldn't think of a single nice thing to say about the baby. She was pink and her mouth kept opening and shutting and she stretched a lot. She was quite interesting to observe, like any life form, really, but she was not 'lovely', which is what people usually said about babies.

'Yous could have told me, though,' he mumbled at last, but nobody seemed to hear him.

'We're going to call her Marguerite,' said Jake's mum. 'After my mother.'

Jake thought about that.

'That's a nice name,' he said carefully, after a while. 'But it doesn't suit her.'

His mother frowned.

'I mean, she's nice and all, but you have to be tall and have a bun if you're called Marguerite.' Not that his grandmother looked like that, but she was always called Rita; Jake hadn't even known her name was Marguerite.

'Mmm,' said his mother dreamily.

'And a silver cigarette case,' Jake added. 'With Russian cigarettes in it.' He smirked, pleased with that touch, though he had no idea what Russian cigarettes were actually like, apart from being cigarettes and Russian.

His mother chuckled softly. He thought it was the Russian cigarettes that had amused her, but then he saw that she hadn't been listening to what he'd said at all. She stroked the baby's palm with her finger, and the baby closed its little fist tightly over the finger, and she chuckled again. It was a soft sound, like music.

'Look how tightly she grips,' she said, as if gripping tightly was some sort of extraordinary talent. But Jake knew that all babies did that. He'd read about it. Theirs wasn't anything special.

'What about Madge?' asked Jake. 'Just till she's older and gets a bun.'

'No,' said his mother. 'Definitely not Madge.' As if Madge meant something horrific, like Virus or Plague or Destruction.

'Or Margie? Maggie? Like in *The Simpsons*.'

'No.'

'Midge? Midge suits her, doesn't it? I mean, she's dead small, isn't she?'

'Stop, Jake.'

'Meg? Meg's nice. Or Meggie? Peggy?'

'No,' said his mother. She had that anxious look again. 'I thought you'd be pleased, Jake.'

'I am,' he said. 'She's class.'

That was a bit of an exaggeration, but she was better than a tropical fish anyway, he'd grant that. Not much better, but she'd improve. They get more interesting, babies, whereas tropical fish stay at the gawping stage forever. Even tadpoles get more interesting, come to think of it.

He thought he wouldn't say that to his mother, though. She might take it the wrong way. She wouldn't like to have her offspring compared to the juvenile stages of pond life, however interesting Jake might think them. Mothers were like that. They seemed to imagine that human babies, and especially *their* human babies, were somehow endowed with a fascination that had nothing to do with the inherent interestingness of the life cycle.

9

He met the girl again. The one who'd been at the bus stop before, the thin one. 'Met' wasn't exactly the word for it. She was in the supermarket, and so was he. He'd stopped at the fish counter to admire the mackerel, all striped and shiny and neatly packed into their skins without a pucker or a ruck, and he noticed her at the next counter, buying salami. She seemed to do a lot of shopping. She was buying a pile of salami. There must be loads of people in her family.

There were, he realized then. The smaller children were with her again, only they had multiplied. There were dozens of them. Well, four. Their hair was all soft and springy-looking and no-coloured, but it hadn't been combed, so it sat like tousled nests on their heads. Some of them had knitted cardigans on, and their shorts were long, for shorts, and very pale, as if they had been washed a lot. Three of them wore pink plastic sandals and one wore blue wellingtons. The girl herself wore a sundress with a flouncy skirt and flip-flops, but it was cold in the supermarket because of the food, and Jake shivered just looking at her, even though he was wearing a thick sweater that one of his grandmothers had brought him back from a holiday and had a picture of a football stadium – unidentified – on it.

He was supposed to be buying nappies for Marguerite. He moved away from the fish counter, and went looking for the baby things.

'Newborn,' his mother had said.

'I know that,' he'd said. What kind of an idiot did she take him for?

'No, I mean, it's a size,' his mother had explained. 'The smallest.'

'Oh,' he said. 'All right.'

But there weren't any 'Newborn' that he could see, only sizes that seemed to go by weight. He wondered what Marguerite weighed. Not a lot was about the best estimate he could manage. They didn't do nappies in 'not a lot', though.

'How old is it?' said a voice beside him.

'What?' he asked, startled, and spun around.

It was the girl again.

'The *baby*,' she said.

'Oh, nought, I suppose,' he said, reddening. 'I mean, it's not old enough to have an age.'

The girl stared at him. Her eyes were mostly pupil, huge black pools, fringed with yellowy green, not the sort of colour eyes usually are. Cat's eyes, he thought.

'They all have an age,' she said evenly. 'You count it in months before they get to one, or in weeks when they're very new.' She spoke extra clearly, as if she thought he might be a bit thick.

'Newborn,' Jake said promptly.

'Then you count it in days,' the girl said. 'But there aren't any "Newborn". You'll have to ask.'

'Ask!'

Jake was horror-stricken. It had been embarrassing enough to have to get the wretched things, but he'd planned on doing it in manly silence, just picking up the packet and marching nonchalantly to the cash desk. He hadn't reckoned on needing to have a conversation about it, with an adult he'd never met.

'Or you could get the next size and hope for the best,' the girl went on. 'Even if they don't fit, they soon will, so it won't be a waste. Is it yours?'

Jake blushed bright red. 'Of course not,' he said. 'I'm only eleven.'

She burst out laughing. Her teeth were small and even and he could see right down her throat when she threw her head back.

'I didn't mean *that*!' she said when she'd got over the first gale of laughter. 'I meant, is it in your family? But I suppose it must be, or they wouldn't have asked you to get the nappies. Boy or girl?

Oh, dear,' she added as she went off into another fit of laughter. She wiped a tear apologetically from her face. Her skin was very pale, and she had freckles, but they were very pale too, so pale you didn't notice unless you looked at her face closely under the harsh lights of a supermarket.

'Girl,' he muttered. 'Marguerite.'

'I see,' said the girl, sobering up. 'What weight is she?'

Weight, weight, what's all this obsession with weight? Jake wondered. It's not as though you could eat babies or had to carry them in your arms over mountains. Who cares what weight it is? It's going to change all the time anyway, not like the weight of a litre of water, which stays comfortingly static.

He shrugged.

'Well, look,' said the girl, losing interest, 'I have to go. Take those ones, you can't go wrong with them.' She thrust a brightly coloured packet at Jake and yelled at the top of her voice at the same time: 'Come on, Dalys!' The children in the cardigans and shorts materialized magically and gathered around her.

'I'd call her Daisy if I were you,' the girl said as she swung her supermarket basket on to a bony hip. 'You have to be beautiful for Marguerite. Daisy will do for just pretty.'

She was gone before he got a chance to ask her

own name. 'Or even plain,' she added, walking away from him.

'At a pinch,' he thought he heard her say, but he couldn't see her. She must be in the next aisle.

What did she mean?

Was she suggesting that their baby wasn't beautiful?

She had no right! What did she know about their baby? Nothing. Not a thing.

10

His mother didn't seem to mind that he'd bought the wrong size of nappies. In fact, Jake thought she hadn't even noticed. Just goes to show what a lot of nonsense it all is, he thought, all that weight stuff.

'What would you think of Daisy?' his mother asked, opening the packet. 'Mmm,' she added, sniffing the clean smell of the fresh nappy.

Daisy! That's what the girl had suggested. Jake jumped guiltily, as if his mother had caught him doing something he shouldn't have been doing, or thinking something he shouldn't have been thinking.

'Daisy?' he managed to squeak out. 'What made you think of that?'

'Mrs O'Dea was here,' his mother said. 'You know, the large woman who runs the garden centre and smokes too much? She brought me a potted marguerite, for luck, she said, because of the baby's name, and it turns out it's one of those big daisies.

Isn't it pretty? All sort of smiley. So I thought, Daisy. For everyday, I mean. She can be Marguerite on her birth cert, of course, and her passport.'

'Yeah,' said Jake, pouring himself a glass of milk. 'Whatever.'

'Oh, Jake, I hope you're not . . . I don't know, going to be *difficult*?'

'I'm not,' said Jake, reaching up for the ginger biscuits, which his mother always deliberately put slightly too high up, so that people wouldn't scoff too many of them. 'You know I'm not. I just mean, it's your choice. It's nice. Daisy's nice. What does Dad think?'

Dad loved Daisy. The name, the child. He was, in short, besotted. Jake had never seen him like this before about anything. He woke her up when he came home from work, just so he could look at her. He fished her feet out of her Babygro and kissed the soles of them and the tiny ankle bones. That made her squirm. Her squirming made him laugh. She squirmed, he laughed, they were happy together. He pressed the tip of her nose with the ball of his thumb, as if he were ringing a doorbell, and she opened her eyes wide in surprise and waved her fingers around like little starfish arms.

Jake pressed his own nose experimentally, to see what it felt like. He wondered if anyone had ever done that to him. He couldn't imagine it.

11

Jake looked up 'Daisy' in the library. He'd looked up 'Marguerite' before, and found it meant 'pearl', which had seemed completely wrong. 'Daisy' was more down to earth.

'The word "daisy" comes from "day's eye",' he told his parents that evening. 'Did you know that?'

'Of course,' said Jake's mum. She always knew everything, a bit like Jake, come to think of it.

'Why?' Dad asked. He could never work things out for himself. Jake sometimes wondered how he didn't get fired from that job of his.

'Because it opens up in the morning and closes at night,' said Jake. 'Those little white petals, just like eyelashes.'

The baby cried. She often did, and she seemed to make a point of doing it when Jake had an interesting conversation going.

'She doesn't get it,' Jake said resentfully. 'About closing at night, I mean. Somebody should tell her to start living up to her name.'

12

Jake had been to the park to kick a ball around with Finn and a few of the lads, and when he got home he had that hot, heavy feeling you get in your feet when you've been running around, and you just want to kick off your shoes, drink a pint of something cold and then stand under a cool shower and gasp as the water pours over your head and trickles down your shoulders.

But – there *she* was, the greyhound girl with the very pale freckles, in the kitchen, drinking a glass of milk and talking to his mother. And eating ginger biscuits, he noticed. The whole tin was on the kitchen table.

'Oh, Jake,' said his mother. She had Daisy in her arms. 'Stella here just called by to see Daisy.'

Stella. Jake registered the name dully.

He took a ginger biscuit, with a defiant look at his mother.

'Hi, Jake,' said Stella, as if they were old friends. 'I was just saying to your mum how you'd been telling me all about Daisy the other day, you know, in the supermarket?'

'Er, yes,' said Jake uncertainly.

'So here I am,' she finished, as if that explained everything.

It didn't, of course. How had she found out where he lived? Had she followed him? Been *watching* him? He looked at her suspiciously. She must have been. There was no other explanation. It made him feel prickly under his football shirt.

He gulped. 'Well . . .' he started, but he didn't know how to continue. He couldn't think of a thing to say in this absurd situation. 'I have to feed the fish,' he said eventually, and he left the kitchen and pounded upstairs.

He didn't come down again till he heard the front door thudding. By then he'd fed the fish (they didn't need feeding), had his shower, dried his hair with his mum's hairdryer (he never did that), changed his clothes and started to tidy his desk (he never did that either).

'You never mentioned your friend before,' his mother said, when he reappeared in the kitchen.

'She's not my friend.'

'Oh, don't be like that, Jake. It's all right to have a friend who's a girl. They're not poison, you know. They haven't got a disease. You'll work it out soon enough, I suppose.'

'She's not my friend,' he persisted. 'What did you say her name was?'

'Jake!'

'Stella, was it?'

'Jake, that's not funny.'

'Mum, I'm telling you, I don't *know* her.'

His mother stared. 'That's funny,' she murmured.

'Yeah, we-eird,' said Jake, relieved that at last he was being believed. 'I saw her in the super-market, we said about three sentences to each other, and next thing she's in my kitchen! How did she know where I live? That's what I want to know. She's some sort of a witch. How did she know my name? We weren't introduced, you know.'

'Oh, Jake, she's not a witch. She just likes babies. Some girls are like that. She got an inkling of a baby in the neighbourhood, and she turned up on the doorstep. It's not that peculiar. And I probably mentioned your name. Though, come to think of it, she knew Daisy's name. Did you tell her that?'

'No,' said Jake. 'It was a few days ago. She was still Marguerite then. That's odd, Mum. You have to admit that's, like, strange?'

'Well, she's a nice enough girl. Though I have to say, that *dress*, in this *weather*.'

'It's June, though,' said Jake, suddenly changing sides. His mother had that effect on him sometimes.

'Theoretically,' said his mother.

She was so illogical.

'No!' said Jake. 'It's *actually* June. Not theoretically.'

'You know what I mean. The weather's dreadful.'

'It's weird about the name, though,' Jake said. 'Maybe we should go back to calling her Marguerite. Just to be on the safe side.'

'We can't do that. I've got to like Daisy. Anyway, we can't keep changing her name. She'd get confused.'

'Mum, she's a week old!'

'Ten days. And she knows her name,' his mother insisted. 'She turns her head when I call her. Watch! Daisy, Daisy?'

The baby turned her head and stared a big wet blue stare at her mother. She parted her lips and blew a soft bubble.

'See?' said his mother triumphantly.

Jake shook his head. Mothers were so unscientific. Or maybe it was poets.

'Oh, she left her address,' his mother said suddenly, producing a crumpled piece of lined paper, torn out of a copybook, out of her pocket.

'Her address?'

'Yes, she said you'd be wanting it.'

'I *don't* want it!' said Jake, pushing the scrap of paper across the table, as if it was infected.

'Well, neither do I,' said his mother. 'I've only just met the girl. Put it in the bin, if you don't want it.'

Jake picked it up reluctantly by one corner, using

his nails, and held it at arm's length. He couldn't help noticing what it said, all the same. She had very clear, flowing handwriting, and she wrote in large, black letters – not like most girls, who went in for mauve and silver and wrote tiny little swirly words, like snails, and put little circles instead of dots over their 'i's. Her address was almost the same as his. They were in Mount Gregor Road; she was in Mount Gregor *Park*. In number ten – same house number as them.

Funny that, he thought, as he stepped down hard on the bin pedal and dropped the paper in on top of eggshells and coffee grounds and a nappy neatly rolled up and wrapped in a drawstring nappy bag.

13

Well, you can't forget somebody's house number if it's the same as your own, can you? Which is how Jake came to be standing outside Stella's house, thinking it looked a bit small for all those children. Just two windows with a door in between and no upstairs. There was a small gate in front, which was closed, and a big one at the side, for cars, which was wide open.

'It's not as small as it looks,' Stella said.

She was doing it again! Witching about the place. Jake spun around.

'I never heard you coming,' he said accusingly.

'Dancing pumps,' she answered, lifting one foot, in a pink ballet shoe, and pointing it in the air. 'Nice, huh? I don't dance, though, I just like the pumps. I got them in the Oxfam shop. I wouldn't like you to think I'm some sort of ballerina person. I'm more a football sort of person, actually. Not that I have anything against ballerinas, it's just not me. But you have to admit that pink satin shoes are cool. Even a boy can see that, I imagine.'

Jake was just about to say he liked football too, but she took off again before he could get more than a grunt out.

'That's the right word, you know, "pumps", but it's terribly ugly, isn't it? I am in a dilemma about it.'

Jake stared at her. What was she on about?

'I mean,' Stella went on, 'I like to use the right word when I know what it is, but I don't like using ugly words. That's the dilemma, you see. Dilemma's a nice word, I hadn't noticed that before. Do you like it?'

Jake went on staring. He couldn't think what to say.

'I collect words,' Stella said. 'It's my hobby. But it's a bit like collecting seashells – you can't collect them all, so I only collect the beautiful ones. Like "mackerel", and "plinth", and "obloquy". I try to go by the sounds, not the meanings, but sometimes the meanings do get in the way, like "tryst", for example. I don't know whether I really like that word, or whether it's just the *idea* of it. Do you see what I mean?'

Jake coughed. 'I like mackerel,' he said at last.

'It goes back and back,' Stella said, nodding at the house. 'Like to come in? You could see my word collection if you like. It's in my room.'

'No,' said Jake.

'OK,' said Stella, unexpectedly. She pushed past Jake and opened the gate. Suddenly, there were children everywhere: two swung out of a tree in the front garden; two tumbled out of the front door, squawking gleefully. One waddled around the side of the house, a small one, barefoot and wearing nothing but a nappy and a blue cotton sun hat, and stared at Jake.

Stella skipped up a couple of shallow steps and on to the garden path. When she got to the front door, she turned and waved at Jake. 'Bye so,' she called.

'Bye,' said Jake, crestfallen, and watched as she scooped the smallest child up and swung him on to a bony hip, then pushed the door wide open. The children all swarmed around her and she touched each one lightly on the head, as if counting them. The children piled in the door, and the house gobbled up their delighted squabblings. The door closed behind them, and the air was full of an uncanny silence.

Jake stared at the door. Then he shrugged and turned away.

14

Jake's mum sat in her study in her dressing gown in the mornings and tried to write. Nothing came. That had never happened to her before, she moaned. Always, something came. All her creativity was going into her milk, she said. Jake thought that wasn't a nice thing to say. Women shouldn't talk like that in front of boys. It was embarrassing.

'I wish I smoked,' she said.

'*What!*' Jake was aghast.

'Poets who can't write smoke. It's better than nothing.'

'No, it's not, it gives you cancer,' said Jake darkly. 'And strokes. And heart attacks. And bad breath. And varicose veins. And nightmares.' He just threw in the last one for effect. Also, he was interested to see if she would challenge him on it.

She didn't even notice.

'Oh, don't worry, I'm not going to start now. It's just that it would be something to do. It would be nice to have something to do. With my hands. With my mouth. You know.'

Jake didn't know. It was his feet that gave him trouble when he had nothing to do, not his hands or his mouth. They kept wanting to kick things. Football helped, but sometimes you couldn't play football, like in the middle of the night or in a snowstorm or at Sunday lunch. It was amazing the number of times you couldn't play football, if you set your mind to thinking about it. In school, in church, in any building, actually, come to think of it. On the bus, on the train, at the airport. On Sundays in Scotland. In bed, in the shower, at the swimming pool. And in Jake's back garden, because there was a sunroom at the back of their house with glass panels. Breakable glass panels, as his parents frequently told him. Expensive-to-replace glass panels.

' "The Daisy follows soft the Sun –",' said Jake's mother, ' "And when his golden walk is done – / Sits shyly at his feet." '

'That's *good*, Mum,' said Jake. 'Especially "follows soft the Sun". And "golden walk". That's a day, I suppose. Like the American Indians; they believe the sun walks across the sky, from sunrise to sunset.'

'Of course it's good,' said his mother glumly, banging her head with the palm of her hand. 'Because I didn't write it. That's Emily Dickinson. And before you ask, yes, she's famous, yes, she's dead, no, she's American, but no, she's not an Indian. How amazing, though, about the sun walking across the sky. You know the maddest stuff, Jake.'

Jake smirked, self-satisfied.

'Or she might be Chinese,' he said, 'you know, because of the word for "sun" being the same as the word for "day" in Chinese. Did you know that?'

'You're a rare one,' his mother said with a laugh, and ruffled Jake's hair. 'But she's not Chinese.'

'Don't,' Jake said, pushing her hand away and smoothing down his hair again. He didn't like having tossed hair.

His mother stood up from her desk in her red silk kimono and stretched her arms over her head. The baby cried.

'Drat,' said his mother – not 'brat' as Jake, for one wonderful, awful moment, had thought – and scratched her head. She yawned, catlike, and drifted out of the room in the direction of the cries.

15

Jake found himself walking past number ten, Mount Gregor Park so often over the next few days that he had to admit it wasn't just by chance. For a start, it was a cul-de-sac, which meant it wasn't on the way to anywhere. Something was drawing him. Stella never appeared, though, so if he was going to talk to her – and it seemed to him, when he thought it over, that he must want to talk to her – he was going to have to ring the doorbell.

He stood on the pavement and thought about ringing the doorbell, and what would happen when he did, and who might answer.

In the end, he decided he would just give it a go. But it didn't work. At least, he couldn't hear it, though maybe it rang somewhere deep in the house. Anyway, no one came, so he picked up the snarling lion's head knocker and let it fall heavily against the door.

Almost immediately Stella was there, framed in the doorway.

'Oh, it's you,' she said, neither surprised nor displeased, it seemed, to see him. 'Come in.'

Jake had been rehearsing things to say, such as, 'Would you like to come and play football in the park?' or 'I was just passing and I thought . . .', but he didn't say any of the lame things he'd been practising. He didn't need to. It was as if she'd been expecting him. Anyway, she didn't seem to wonder why he had knocked.

She was right about the house being bigger than it looked. Much bigger. It went on and on, room opening out of room, till you got to the kitchen at the very back, off which was a room called the back kitchen, where they kept wellingtons and garden implements and a vegetable rack full of onions with long browny-green leafy bits, like leeks, and a sack half full of potatoes, and a basket for the dog. They didn't have a dog, just a dog basket. Nobody explained why. Maybe one of the younger ones slept in it, Jake thought, and giggled quietly at his own hilarity.

When you went through the back kitchen, which smelt unpleasantly of onions and rubber, and out into the garden, it went on and on too. You couldn't call it a yard, exactly, because there were quite a lot of things growing in it, like apple trees and grass and cabbages, but there were also a lot of things that didn't belong in a garden – a pram with one wheel missing, several window frames and a rusty washing machine. At the end of the garden was a large shed with a flat roof. This was the studio, Stella said. Her parents were photographers, it seemed, and this was where they worked. There were windows, but black blinds were drawn over them.

Stella's mother appeared at the door of the studio. She was short and sturdy and wore a denim skirt and shirt and had the same no-colour hair as the children, only it was short with bubbly curls.

'Yes?' she said, looking enquiringly at Jake.

She had a bright-red necklace on, one with shiny red beads. It made her look businesslike and jolly at the same time. She looked like a mum in a picture book. Jake thought disloyally of his own mum, with her wild hair and still in her dressing gown at lunchtime.

'It's all right, he's for me,' Stella said.

'Okey-dokey,' said Stella's mother. She gave Jake a smile and went away.

That was a bit *too* jolly, Jake thought, but he'd give her a second chance if he met her again. She might be all right.

It turned out that the doorbell was wired through to the studio, and Stella's mother had thought it was a customer ringing.

'You should put a sign on it,' Jake said, 'so people would know not to ring unless they're on business.'

'Can't,' said Stella. 'The neighbours don't like

the studio being here at all. They'd have us up in court if we put a sign up about it.'

Jake looked over the walls. On either side, the gardens were perfectly tended, with white-painted benches poised under artistically draped apple boughs and little gritted paths edged with white-painted stones. The lawns looked as if they had been shaved and the edges trimmed with nail scissors. In one there was a square wooden archway, festooned with very thorny-looking roses, with flowers as big as cabbages. In the other was a small kidney-shaped pond with a concrete heron standing guard over it and a lot of water lilies.

'I see,' he said.

'Daisy-murderers,' muttered Stella fiercely.

Jake barked a laugh. She meant the kind that grow in the grass, of course, and follow soft the sun.

'Mrs Peacock,' he said darkly, 'in the Garden, with the Lawnmower.'

Stella stared. 'Oh,' she said at last. 'That's a game, isn't it? Detectives or something. I'm not much good at cards.'

'Mm,' said Jake. 'It's a board game, not a card game. Do you think there might be fish in that pond?'

'I never saw any, but then you wouldn't, would you? Unless you had a telescope.'

'Will we investigate?' Jake suggested.

'Why?' asked Stella.

'I like fish,' said Jake.

'We will, then,' said Stella gamely.

The garden wall was rather high and smooth for climbing, but at one end of the garden, growing almost against the wall, on Stella's side, was a muscular-looking cherry tree, so they climbed that first, and stepped off it on to the wall. From there it was a steep jump down into the next-door garden. Stella closed her eyes and held her nose, as if she were jumping off a diving board, and over she went. Jake watched her folding herself into a comma shape in the air, and landing all curled up on the lawn next door.

Not to be outdone, he leapt off the wall, arms flailing, and landed in an untidy heap beside her.

Giggling softly, they rolled on to their bellies and started to work their way, using their elbows and their knees, like ungainly lizards, over the lawn towards the pond, keeping low and out of sight.

When they got to the edge of the pond, they stared into the water. It was green and opaque and insects buzzed quietly over its brackish surface. It smelt old, like hundreds of years.

Something moved in the dark and greeny water and Jake screwed up his eyes. Something orange, he thought, the merest flicker of brightness in the murk. Yes! A goldfish, a large one, drifting slowly in the shade of the water lilies.

'Fish are boring,' Stella hissed, after a while. 'They do nothing except wiffle around.'

'That's the whole point of fish,' Jake said. 'That's why they're so great. They don't bother with humans, just get on with . . . wiffling around. But anyway, that's not what I call a real fish.'

'Of course it's real. You can't get fake fish. Can you? Why would anyone want to?'

'Listen!' Jake said.

Shuffle, stomp.

They froze. The sound was distant, but it was coming nearer. Shuffle, stomp. Shuffle, stomp.

'It's a hippopotamus,' Jake whispered. 'Coming back to the waterhole.'

'Or a water buffalo,' Stella breathed.

Their bodies shook with laughter.

'It's Mrs Peabody,' hissed Stella, 'the serial daisy-murderess.'

'Mrs Peacock,' Jake corrected her. 'The people are all called after colours in Cluedo.'

'Peacock is a bird,' whispered Stella, 'not a colour.'

'It's a colour too,' said Jake. 'Like orange, only that's a fruit, of course.'

'Of course,' snorted Stella, and stuffed her fist into her mouth to keep from laughing out loud.

Shuffle, stomp.

They were going to be caught, whoever it was, but they couldn't think of anything to do except lie there and wait.

'It's a grampus,' said Jake wildly.

'A geyser,' said Stella, spitting grass out of her mouth.

'It's a walrus,' said Jake, louder than he meant to. The sounds were very close now, but he couldn't help himself.

'It's an old lady with arthritis,' said a voice from above them, sounding very like an old lady with arthritis.

Slowly Jake and Stella turned over and looked up, blinking into the light.

'You're from the bus stop,' said Jake, when he finally managed to focus.

'I'm from Cork,' said the old lady, and leant on her aluminium walking stick with three funny legs with rubber feet on the bottom. 'A bus stop is no sort of a place for a respectable person to be from. Stand up, the pair of ye. I can't talk to a couple of snakes in the grass.'

Sheepishly, Jake and Stella stood up and half-heartedly brushed themselves down.

'That dress is ruined,' said the old lady with arthritis, lowering herself carefully on to a convenient garden bench. 'Grass stains don't come out. Your mother will be cross.'

'She won't,' said Stella. 'She doesn't get cross. Anyway, she has a special magic soap.'

'Remarkable,' said the old lady with arthritis, and rested her chin on her hands, which rested on the top of her aluminium stick.

'He says your goldfish is fake,' Stella said, to fill the silence.

'I don't mean fake, exactly,' said Jake. 'I just mean, not natural. Like my tropical fish. It's as if they're in costume. Pretending to be fish. Acting.'

'I see,' said the old lady with arthritis. 'I quite follow. So what kind of fish do you consider to be real?'

Jake thought for a moment.

'Silvery ones,' he said at last.

'Ah, yes,' she said. 'Yes, that's good. Very good. And who, by the way, might you be?'

'I'm Jake,' Jake said, and then, thinking that sounded a bit blunt, he added, by way of extending the introduction, 'I'm going to be a fish painter. That's why I was looking in your pond.'

'A fish painter, I see. When you grow up?'

She was the first grown-up who had ever seen. Jake looked at her admiringly.

'Yes,' he said.

'I'm Stella. I live next door. I'm going to be a lexicographer.'

'I know your face. I know your mother.'

'But you don't live here,' said Stella, 'because this is Mr Kennedy's house, and his wife is young. For an adult, I mean.'

'Indeed,' said the old lady with arthritis. 'As you can see, this is not a garden that is tended by an old lady with arthritis. My son lives here, he and his wife. He is Mr Kennedy, though I do not usually think of him like that. I think of him as Seán. I live here now too, but I've only just moved in. The new girl, you might say.'

Stella and Jake didn't say anything to that. They were wondering if they could reasonably leave sometime soon.

In the end, the old lady closed her eyes and seemed to want to sleep, so they just tiptoed away, climbed over the wall – with some difficulty, since there was no helpful cherry tree on this side – and launched themselves back into Stella's garden.

16

'What's a lexic . . . that thing you want to be when you grow up?' Jake asked Stella. They were in her room, and he was staring at her word collection. The words were all written out in large black flowing letters on strips of plain white paper, and they were pinned to the walls. The whole room was covered in them, like fluttery wallpaper.

'Oh, that's just a dream,' said Stella. 'I don't think there will be any by the time I grow up. It'll all be done by computers.'

'But what is it?'

'Making dictionaries,' Stella said.

'You could always be a poet,' Jake said. 'If there are no jobs for lexithingies.'

'No, I couldn't,' said Stella. 'I only collect them. I can't make them rhyme.'

'You don't need to make them rhyme,' Jake said.

'Of course you do.'

'No, you don't. Lots of poetry doesn't rhyme.

Rhyme is out of date . . . some people think . . . so I hear.'

'How come you know so much about poetry?' Stella asked.

'I know about lots of things,' said Jake. 'Do you like fishing?'

He only asked to change the subject, but that was just the right question, as it turned out.

17

Jake's mother loved it when people came to admire Daisy. She threw open the front door and made wide gestures with her arms when she heard why Stella had come. She looked a little less enthusiastic when Stella's siblings appeared out of nowhere, in that startling way they had, and started to fill the hall with their murmelings and squawkings and the soft patter of their flip-flopped and sandalled feet.

'I thought she was supposed not to be your friend,' his mother hissed at Jake.

'That was last week,' Jake said. 'But I found out she likes fishing.'

'And what about the others? There's millions of them!'

'They'll be OK,' said Jake, sounding surer than he felt. The younger ones hadn't been part of the deal. The deal was, first a quick visit to Daisy, and then they were going fishing – he and Stella, as far as Jake was concerned. It hadn't crossed his mind that it was going to be a family outing. But he wasn't going to let on about this to his mother. 'They mostly play quietly together.'

He hoped that was true, and it was. Roughly.

They trooped into Jake's kitchen and they sat under the table, and, for a little while, there wasn't a squeak out of them. Then suddenly the table started to rock, and muffled sounds came from under it.

Jake's mother looked alarmed as some stray cutlery that was lying on the tabletop started to slither about, but Stella lifted the brightly patterned oilcloth that Jake's mother liked to cover the table with and asked them, in a calm voice, what they were playing.

'Boats,' said one.

'Tents,' said another.

'OK,' said Stella, 'but hush up a bit, OK?' She let the tablecloth fall again.

That seemed to settle them. It was amazing the effect Stella had on them.

'They're just playing,' she said. 'They'll be good as gold.'

'I hope you're not taking all those children fishing with you,' said Jake's mother in a worried voice. 'They might fall in.'

'Oh, not at all,' said Stella. 'Of course not.'

Jake's mother looked relieved.

18

Jake's idea of fishing was to put a worm on a hook, sling it over the pier and hope for the best. Stella had a more complicated approach. She squinted at the horizon, licked her finger and held it up in the wind and squinched her face into a monkey's snout while she appeared to smell the tide.

Jake stared at her, and then he stared at the younger children, who all sat in a row on the pier and worked quickly and quietly, untangling Stella's fishing gear. There was masses of it, things called spinners and bobs and flies – all things Jake had never even heard of – bundled into a biscuit box.

'How come they're doing that?' Jake asked, nodding towards the working children.

'I promised them ice creams if they're good.'

'That's bribery,' said Jake.

'Fair exchange is no robbery,' said Stella, whatever that was supposed to mean.

'Where's the small one?' Jake asked suddenly,

looking around. 'Did we leave him on the DART? Oh, my God!'

'No,' said Stella. 'He's Fergal. He stays at home. He's too young.'

'For fishing?'

'For me,' said Stella. She was gouging a limpet out of its shell with her penknife. Then she sliced it in two and gave Jake one piece, for bait.

'I don't do small ones,' she said. 'I mean, I love them to bits, but I don't mind them until they're old enough not to fall in. Or nearly.' She nodded towards the youngest one she had with her, whose name seemed to be Joey, only it was wearing a dress, which didn't seem quite right.

Jake looked dubiously at the children who were supposed to be old enough not to fall in. He didn't for a moment think they were all that specially trustworthy, even if they had played quietly – fairly quietly – under his kitchen table for a good half-hour. They pranced about a bit too much, in his view. Their feet seemed to be on a level with their ears more often than he was entirely happy about.

'I thought you told my mother that we weren't bringing them with us.'

'No,' said Stella. 'That's not what I said. I said they wouldn't fall in. And they won't.'

'Does *your* mother know they're here?'

'That's none of your business, Jake,' said Stella.

66

'It will be if one falls in,' said Jake in a worried voice.

Stella just laughed at him.

They sat for long hours on the pier and held their fishing rods, and had pointless, pleasant conversations. They caught four mackerel – pretty small ones, but still – also, something Jake thought might be a pollack and a very ugly thing they didn't know the name of and threw back. The younger children played running-up-and-down-and-not-falling-in, all except for Joey, who seemed quite happy to sit quietly by Stella's side as long as Stella let her hold the rod from time to time.

There was a lot to be said for being an only child, Jake thought, watching the others running up and down.

Then he remembered. There was this huge thing in his life, so huge that he couldn't even keep it in his head. He wasn't an only child any more. He wondered what the daisies did on cool days like this. Snoozed, perhaps. Which was probably what Daisy was doing right now. Babies really were not all that terribly interesting.

And then one fell in.

There was a yelp, and a splash, and everyone rushed to the edge and pointed.

Jake didn't stop to think. He leapt in after the child. Fully clothed. He didn't even stop to take off his runners.

The water was freezing, black and cold and deep, deep, and hitting it was like being punched hard in the chest by huge, swaying punchbags of ice. Jake was a strong swimmer, but he shivered as he sank into the blackness and his body filled with cold. He came up, gasping painfully, for air and opened his streaming eyes.

It hurt to open his eyes, and it hurt to keep them closed. He blinked and gasped and pushed his salt-dank hair back off his forehead with the flat of his hand. For a moment, everything seemed out of focus, blurred. He couldn't think why he was so cold, he couldn't imagine what he was doing in this freezing sea, everything was indistinct, as if he were miles away from everything around him, on some different plane of reality. Everything was fractured, disjointed, swirling colours and shapes sped away from him, distant, shrieking snatches of sound spun around him, and nothing made sense.

He felt himself being dragged down by the weight of . . . by the weight of what? He trod water desperately and examined himself, panic-stricken, and found he was dressed, dressed and streaming, and his feet felt like sinkers.

Suddenly the world coalesced around him, rifts of sound and streaks of light rushing together to form suddenly recognizable images of the world again, and he knew where he was and why. It could only have been for a moment that he had been 'gone', but in that time the child – oh, no, the child! – could have drowned.

Jake flailed out desperately, in another wave of panic, beginning to feel himself slipping out of reality again, into a dreamy, bubbling, slow-motion world where images crazed and cracked and dispersed, where his senses seemed to lose contact with his brain.

Afterwards, he could piece it together only dimly. He must somehow have registered the small pale-haired head in the water, his brain must have clocked it and sent him swimming in the right direction, but he had no awareness of what he was doing. He was aware only of pain and endlessly passing time. He found that he was swimming, apparently purposefully, apparently in a particular direction, and he followed himself, so to speak, swimming on in the direction that he seemed to have mapped out for himself. He could think of nothing now but his own strenuous swimming. It was as if he was scooping up the whole bay in his arms with every stroke, and shifting it forcibly aside, to make room for his body, and then with the next stroke, he embraced the whole black bay again.

Something whizzed over his head and landed with a resounding plop a few feet in front of him, like a messenger from the real world. Jake looked at it for a moment, swimming gingerly towards it, not recognizing it, and then he twigged. It was a lifebelt. He thought something incoherent, but he must have done something sensible, because the next thing he could remember, afterwards, was swimming back towards the pier, dragging something behind him, and when he looked over his shoulder to check, it was indeed a small child, somehow affixed to a lifebelt that he had no memory of attaching to it. It must be dead, Jake remembered thinking. If it were alive, it would be screeching and resisting.

Nothing made sense, only the cold and the rush of the water in his ears and the painful gulping sensation in his chest. That was himself, breathing, he realized. He had no idea where he was going, but he seemed to be aware of Stella. He couldn't see or hear her, but he had the sensation of swimming towards her and gradually he began to focus again and now he could actually see and hear her, on the pier presumably, dancing and waving frantically, pointing to something. He followed the line of her arm. He could see nothing, but he swam in the direction she pointed in anyway.

Oh joy! A steel ladder was set into the side of the pier, the bottom of it disappearing under the surface of the water. A man – a man? – was clinging to the ladder, one arm reaching out to Jake. Jake swam towards him.

'Come on, lad,' came a voice. 'You're doing

70

great, almost there. Pass her up to me. And thanks, oh, thanks, thanks, thank you.'

Then came another medley of sensations, sinking, bobbing up again, spluttering, losing control, catching on to something solid, the feeling of something slippery and lithe being wrenched from his grasp, and then he was hauled, hauled, yanked and winched, or so it seemed, up and out of the water and on to solid ground.

He had never felt so heavy in all his life. His clothes and hair and shoes were full of seawater, which weighed him down, but that wasn't the reason. It was being back on dry land after the weightlessness of swimming. He lay on his back and closed his eyes. He could feel hands pulling his shoes off, people breathing on his face, something hot being pressed against his lips. He pushed it away. All he wanted to do was sleep.

19

'I'm sorry,' said Jake, when he woke up.

He was warm. All over. Even his toes felt rosy.

'What do you mean?' asked Stella. Her face was close to his. 'What do you mean, you're sorry?'

'About your little sister,' Jake said. 'She's dead, isn't she?'

Stella turned her head and looked around.

'No,' she said. 'Definitely not. All my sisters are here, and they are all very much alive. Thank goodness. My mother will have my life as it is.'

Jake's heart leapt.

Then it sank.

'Well, your brother, then. For goodness' sake, Stella, I didn't have time to check whether it was male or female! I did think it was a girl, though.'

'My brother? Fergal's at home with my parents. I told you that before,' Stella said.

Jake processed this information. The brother was at home – there was only one, it seemed; and the sisters were all alive.

'Well, that's good,' Jake said, pleased. 'Will she make a full recovery?'

'Who?' asked Stella in a puzzled voice.

'Whatever her name is,' said Jake. Really, this conversation was wearing him out. 'Your sister.' It hurt his chest to talk.

'Which sister, Jake?'

'How would I know?' Jake snapped. 'Whichever one fell in.' It was such an effort to talk. It was as if his upper and lower jaws belonged to two different faces, neither of them his.

Stella laughed.

'Oh, lordy,' she said, and laughed again. 'Oh, hi-cockalorum, cockalee!'

Jake closed his eyes. He couldn't cope with it. And where had she got that cackling expression from?

'Jake,' Stella said, and she touched his cheekbone lightly with her finger. 'Jake, can you hear me?'

Jake kept his eyes closed, but he nodded.

'Jake, it wasn't my sister who fell in. I told you, they don't fall in. It was some other child. Nuala Something. Her silly parents let her wander off, and she just wandered a bit too far. But she's fine. Thanks to you. She's only a teeny tiny, and she was so young, she didn't even know to panic, which is why you were able to rescue her without being pulled down yourself.'

Jake couldn't listen any longer. He wondered if Stella had bought the ice creams for the younger children, but he didn't really want to think about ice cream. It made his face ache to think about anything cold. He closed his eyes again and drifted off into a grateful sleep.

20

When he woke up the next time, his mother was there.

'Well, if it isn't the hero!' she said, when she saw his eyelids flutter open.

Jake grinned. 'I thought it was Stella's sister,' he croaked. His throat felt as if he had been eating brambles.

'I know,' said his mum, 'but I suppose you would have jumped in anyway, even if you'd known it was just some other nipper.'

'Well, I don't know,' said Jake. 'I suppose.'

'You shouldn't have done it, you know,' his mother said. 'You should have called the lifeguard and thrown out a lifebelt. That's what the other people on the pier did. And if you really needed to go in, you should have got your kit off first.'

'Yeah,' said Jake. 'I suppose. I'm hot, Mum. I'm baking.'

'That's because you're wrapped in tinfoil,' his mother said, 'and they have been reverse-hoovering you with hot air. Your temperature went way down. You were like a fish. You still are, I suppose. Baked fish!'

'What's reverse-hoovering?'

'You know, like a hairdryer, blowing air out instead of sucking it in. It's terribly interesting to watch.'

'You could write a poem about it,' Jake said faintly.

'Maybe I could.'

'My tummy hurts,' Jake said. His jaws both seemed to belong to him at this stage. That was a big improvement. But his stomach felt as if someone had walked over it in hobnailed boots.

'They had to get the seawater out,' his mother said.

Jake shuddered. 'Don't tell me any more,' he said. 'I don't want to think about it.'

His mother's hair was everywhere as usual. He put out his hand and fingered it lightly. His mother smiled at him and kissed him on the forehead, the way she used to do when he was a little boy.

He smiled back.

'Nuala's mum and dad want to talk to you,' she whispered. 'Do you think you're up to it?'

'*Who?*'

'The little girl that you rescued, her parents. They're dying to meet you and thank you. They think you're wonderful. It was her dad who pulled her out of the water, out of your arms. He told me about it over and over again. He thinks you're a star. He kept saying so. He's very excitable, but I suppose you can understand.'

'Oh, so that's why he said thanks,' Jake said. 'Do I have to see them? What'll I say?'

'I think you could let them do the talking,' Jake's mother said.

'Are you sure she's OK, Naomi, Noelle, whatever her name is?'

'Nuala,' said his mother. 'Yes, they've wrapped her up like a baked fish too. She's in another cubicle somewhere.'

'OK then,' said Jake. 'Send in the fans.'

21

'That's my boy!' said Jake's dad when they got home. He'd already heard the whole story of the rescue. Someone must have phoned him. 'That's my boy!'

It was the best thing his dad had ever said to him. It made Jake feel all shivery up and down, strange inside and shivery up and down.

'It was nothing,' he said, embarrassed.

But it was something. He knew that.

'That's my boy,' said Dad again, with this huge beam across his face. 'But I hope you never do it again! You . . . you might have drowned, Jake.'

His voice sounded cracked.

Jake felt shivery all over again.

You could get to like that shivery feeling, he thought. Quite different from the shivers you get from half-freezing to death in the sea.

But now all he wanted was to wash the salt out of his hair and off his skin, and then to sleep and sleep.

22

Two cards came for Jake.

The first one was a get-well card, which he thought was odd, since he wasn't sick, just a bit shaken. His mother made him go to bed in the afternoons for a couple of days, to 'get your strength back', but he wasn't sick. He didn't mind going to bed, though, because his mother had put a small television in his room, 'just while you're . . .', and there was Wimbledon in the afternoons. It would have been better if the European championships had still been on, but now there was Wimbledon, which wasn't as exciting but was much better than looking at the ceiling.

The card was from Mr and Mrs O'Halloran, 'Nuala's parents', it said in brackets, and inside it was a cheque for fifty euro, 'to buy yourself something nice, with our thanks'.

'That's lovely,' Jake's mum said. 'We'll put it in your savings account, till you decide what to do with it.'

Jake's mum was very fond of putting money in his savings account. Anyone would think it was *her* savings account, the interest she took in it.

The other card was a postcard. It had a painting of a dead fish on the front, by somebody with a strange name beginning with 'van'. Jake's mother said that meant the painter was Dutch. There were other things in the picture too, grapes and a tin plate and a jug of wine, but the main thing – the best thing – was the fish. Its skin shimmered with silvery lights and its head pointed magnificently.

'Hear you've been fishing for compliments, so here's one: Well done!' was the message. There was a squiggly signature, but all Jake could make out were the initials: MK.

He got the shivery feeling again when he read it, only not as strongly as when his dad had said, 'That's my boy.'

'What sort of a fish is it?' asked Stella, when she came to visit.

'I don't know,' Jake said. 'Whiting maybe, they're lovely and silvery. I wonder how she knew my address.'

'Who?'

'MK. Mrs Kennedy. You know.'

'No, I don't know any Mrs Kennedys. And I don't think people put M for Mrs in their signatures.'

'It could be M for Maureen, though. Or Myra, or Miriam, or Molly, or Mairéad.'

'Do you mean our Mr Kennedy next-door's wife?' Stella asked. 'I don't think she's called Mrs Kennedy, though.'

'His mother,' said Jake. 'The old lady with arthritis.'

'What makes you think it's her?' Stella squinched up her eyes, but she couldn't make anything more out of the signature than MK.

'Because she knows I want to be a fish painter.' Stella didn't look convinced.

'Well, make a better suggestion,' Jake said.

'Oh, you're probably right,' said Stella. 'Can I bring my sisters in? To meet you. I mean, formally. You've met them before, but you don't even know their names, and you saved their lives. Sort of. At least, that's what you thought you were doing. They're thrilled. You're their hero.'

'But I didn't save their lives. I possibly saved the life of some other child called Naomi Something. And I'm not a hero. I didn't even think. I wish . . .'

'Oh, do shut up, Jake, dear,' Stella said. 'You're blathering and rawmayshing. And it was Nuala Something.' She opened the get-well card again. 'O'Halloran,' she added.

Jake wasn't used to being called 'dear'. Not even his mother ever called him that. He blushed.

'Where are they?' he said, banging on his pillows to fluff them up and cover his embarrassment.

'Outside the door, waiting.'

'They're not making any noise.'

Stella assumed this meant yes. She opened the door, and in tumbled the nesty-haired quartet.

'This is Isobel,' Stella began. 'Also known as Bella.'

'Hi, Isobel,' said Jake sheepishly. She was the tallest, next to Stella, and she was wearing a sparkly thing in her mussed hair. They all had mussed hair, except Stella, who had a ponytail today. It made her face seem even thinner than normal. Her cheeks were hollow.

'And this is Edel. Also known as Della.'

Jake laughed. 'Stella, Bella, Della! Hi, Edel.'

Edel was the next in size. She gave a deep curtsy, holding out the corners of her bright green skirt. She wore a sparkly thing in her hair too – Jake could see when she bent her head – and she had a flower painted on the back of her hand, or perhaps it was a transfer.

'And this is Danielle,' said Stella.

'Let me guess,' said Jake. 'Also known as Ella.'

'Wrong!' said Danielle. 'Also known as Danny.' She tried to copy Edel's curtsy, but she wasn't very good at it, and anyway, it didn't work so well with dungarees, which is what she was wearing.

'And the little one,' said Stella, 'is Joanne.'

'Joanne!'

'Hi, Dake,' said Joanne.

'Also known as Joey,' Stella added.

'What happened to you?' asked Jake. 'How come your name doesn't match?'

Joanne was too shy to answer, so Stella said, 'Oh, we just got bored with that idea, and anyway, Danielle wouldn't play along, so we gave up on it.'

'What age are you, Joanne?' asked Jake, thinking that was the sort of thing adults usually asked children, and he was so much older than Joanne that he might as well be grown up.

'Theenahaff,' said Joanne, and beamed a big blue-eyed beam at him. 'I go to pwayschoow.'

This was not the kind of information Jake had much experience of dealing with, but he rose to the occasion.

'That's . . . that's just terrific, Joanne,' he said. 'Um . . . what a big girl you are!'

Joanne beamed again and climbed up on to Jake's bed. He moved his legs to make room for her, and she sat happily in the warm space he made.

'Fiss!' she yelped suddenly, spotting the aquarium. 'Oh! Fiss!' She opened her hand into a star and flapped it in the direction of the fish. Then she looked at her other hand, in a fist, and opened it too.

It wasn't just the fish tank. Jake's room was full of fish. Posters of freshwater and sea fish of Ireland. Posters of fish of the world. And one whole wall was covered in drawings and paintings that Jake had done of fish, practising for when he grew up. He didn't think they were much good, but everyone has to start somewhere was his attitude.

'One fiss, two fiss, wed fiss, boo fiss,' Joanne chanted happily, and flapped her starry little hand again at the fish. Then she flapped the other one. Then she flapped them both together.

'She's . . . she's . . .' said Jake.

'Yeah,' said Stella. 'She is, isn't she?'

23

Daisy was sleeping through the night. At least, that's what Jake's mother said. That meant she went to bed at two o'clock in the morning and didn't wake until six.

Big deal, thought Jake. But he kept his mouth shut.

'She belongs to both of you,' he said one day, watching how his mum and dad looked adoringly at the baby. 'You're the perfect little family, aren't you?'

His dad looked at his mum, and his mum looked at his dad, and nobody said anything. The silence was like a wall behind which Jake had trapped himself.

After a while, his mother said, 'She belongs to you too, Jake, and you belong to us. We all belong together.'

Corny, or what? Anyway, that wasn't what he had meant.

He went out and phoned Finn and arranged to

meet him in the park for football. He wasn't going to bed that afternoon, he'd decided. And just let his mother try making him.

He wasn't sick, and he wasn't a hero. He was going back to being just Jake, right now.

24

'My dad's not really my father,' Jake announced to Stella. His heart was flipping madly against the inside of his chest. He'd never told a soul before. It was like a secret that he'd carried around all his life, and took out sometimes when he was alone to examine and have a think about.

They were sitting on the wall, picking cherries off the old cherry tree in Stella's back garden and putting them in an enamel bowl.

Stella's mother was going to make a tart. Someone had given her a cherry stoner for Christmas and she wanted to see if it worked, and you could only justify stoning cherries, she said, if you were going to put them in a tart. So she was. Jake thought this was a funny reason to make a tart. A better reason was that there were so many cherries.

'Hmm?' said Stella. She put a really dark-red cherry to her mouth and bit into it. 'Mmm,' she said. 'Delicious.' Juice dribbled down the side of her mouth when she spoke. She looked like a vampire, very pale, with blood dripping down her chin.

'So?' Jake asked anxiously.

'I'm just thinking about it, Jake,' Stella said. 'It's . . .' – she swallowed – 'interesting.'

'I mean, he is my *dad* of course; I've always called him that. But not my father. My real father disappeared years ago. I never knew him. He just left. My mother says he didn't like babies. That was me, the baby, only there was only one of me, of course, but one was one too many. It was nothing personal, my mum says. Just babies in general drove him mad.'

'Oh, I see. OK.'

Stella spat out the cherry stone and bit into another cherry. Jake stared at her, willing her to say something more.

'That explains why you don't look remotely like him, I suppose, your dad,' she said eventually, sticking her tongue out as far as it would go to lick up the juice from around her mouth. 'Not that I ever thought about it before, but now you mention it, you don't. Look like him, I mean.'

Jake's heart wasn't flipping so wildly now, but it was still going faster than usual. It seemed to fill his chest cavity.

'Well, of course I don't. I've just told you. He's not my father.'

'Of course you don't,' Stella repeated dutifully.

'How could you? Unless it's like dogs and their owners. But it's not, is it?'

'So that's it, then?' Jake said. 'That's all you've got to say?' He didn't know what he'd expected, but he'd thought there'd be more of a reaction than this.

Stella spat out the second cherry stone.

She squinched up her face, in that way she had, and said nothing for a moment. Jake guessed she was thinking.

'Well,' she said at last, 'I suppose you get to have two fathers, so.'

That had never occurred to Jake before. Two fathers. One more than most people. Two more than some people.

Was this necessarily a good thing?

'I suppose,' he said.

'Good for you,' said Stella, and put another cherry in her mouth.

Well . . .

OK then. Good for him.

Yeah.

'And how old were you, you know, when your new dad came along?'

'Oh, I was only a baby. I don't know. Six months?'

'Well then,' said Stella.

'Well then, what?'

'Well then, that hardly counts, does it?'

'What?'

'I mean, he might as well be your father, mightn't he, if he's been there all along, you know? So it hardly counts, does it, that he isn't?'

Jake sighed. She didn't get it.

He gave up trying to explain himself and bit into a cherry.

25

Shuffle, stomp.

Shuffle, stomp.

It was an unmistakable sound.

'Here comes the walrus,' sang Stella softly. She indicated with her head towards the next-door garden.

Jake laughed, and turned around gingerly. He had the bowl of cherries on his lap and he didn't want to topple them.

'Hello, Mrs Kennedy!' he called over his shoulder.

Shuffle, stomp.

'It's Mrs *Peacock*,' Stella muttered, standing up on the wall. 'Remember, she murders daisies.'

'No, she doesn't. She's only the daisy-murderer's mother. Don't be mean about her. I think she's cool.'

'Ah, Jake!' said the old lady with arthritis, looking up through the cherry foliage. 'How do you know my name?'

'Worked it out. Maybe I'll be a detective when I grow up.'

'Instead of a fish painter?'

'Well, if times get bad and I can't sell my paintings. Thanks for the card.'

She smiled. 'Ah, you worked that out too, did you?'

'Couldn't be anyone else,' he said.

'Is what's-her-name there?'

'Stella?'

'I'm here!' Stella called. She was actually *in* the cherry tree now, with one foot on each of two boughs, reaching out for the very darkest, juiciest cherries, from the topmost branches.

'Well, will you come in for some tea, the pair of you?' Mrs Kennedy asked.

'We will,' said Stella's voice from up in the tree. 'We'll be in in five minutes. Will we come over the wall?'

'No, ring the doorbell. There's nobody here, only me. They're all away on holidays, I'm minding the house. It'll take me five minutes to get to the door anyway, so there's no rush. And check with your mother first, Stella. I don't want to be accused of stealing you.'

'We're not worth stealing,' Stella called as she climbed down the cherry tree. 'But I'll tell Mum we're dropping in to you. See you in five!'

'Make it fifteen, actually,' said Mrs Kennedy. 'I have to get things ready, and I'm slow.'

26

'I love your dancing pumps, Stella,' was the first thing Mrs Kennedy said when she opened the door.

Stella grinned and did her pointy thing with her foot in the air. There were pink satin ribbons that went halfway up to her knees and tied in a bow at the side.

'But I hope you weren't climbing trees in them, you'll ruin them.' She seemed to worry a lot about things getting ruined.

'No,' said Stella. 'I changed into them. Specially.'

'Well, I'm flattered, I'm sure,' said Mrs Kennedy. She didn't mention the cherry juice on Stella's white T-shirt, which she hadn't bothered to change.

'We brought you some cherries,' said Jake, offering her a small bowl.

'Ah, what life is not a bowl of,' said Mrs Kennedy. 'Thank you.'

'Excuse me?' said Jake.

'Life is not a bowl of cherries, Jake,' said Mrs Kennedy gravely.

'Oh, I see,' said Jake. 'I knew that, actually.'

'Will you carry them for me, Jake? I can't manage my stick and a bowl of cherries. Come in, come in, children.'

The house was unbelievably tidy and clean and beautiful and very, very still. It reminded Jake of a painting, only you couldn't be actually *in* a painting. There were carpets on the floor – not just one carpet, like in a normal house, but lots of rugs, some of them overlapping, and even Mrs Kennedy's characteristic shuffle-stomping was muffled.

A huge portrait of a very beautiful young girl in an old-fashioned dress and carrying a candle in a candlestick hung on the landing, and looked right down the stairs at everyone who came in the front door. She stared rather sadly at them as they shuffled, stomped, wriggled and jiggled through the hall and into the drawing room.

That's what Mrs Kennedy called it, but there were no drawing things in there, only more over-lapping red rugs with flowers and designs on them, low, cream-coloured sofas and chairs, with large red tasselled cushions flung and heaped in the corners. The air felt thick, warm, and there was a smell of roses. Jake looked around for a vase of roses, but there weren't any that he could see, though there was an embroidered vase of deep-red roses on a funny sort of framed picture that stood in front of the fireplace. It had feet, so it could stand on the hearth and didn't need to be hung or propped up. There was a long stool in front of the fireplace, covered in a red fabric. At least three people could sit on it, side by side. It was nearly as big as a sofa, only without a back. Best of all, the walls were lined with pictures. Paintings, drawings, watercolours, portraits, landscapes, colouredy blobs – all sorts of things. They weren't just in rows, they completely covered the walls.

Stella looked around her, awestruck. 'I can't believe this house is next door to ours,' she said. 'You should see our living room, Mrs Kennedy. There's no carpet, because you can't tricycle on carpet; we took it up long ago, and my dad made the mistake of painting the floor a sort of apple green – it's pretty revolting. There's hardly any furniture either.'

'That'd be because of the tricycling too, I suppose,' said Mrs Kennedy.

'Partly,' said Stella, 'but I think it just got broken, bit by bit, and got thrown out. We have a very large, square coffee table, and a lot of beanbags. We sit on the coffee table if we don't want to sit in the beanbags, though we're not supposed to.'

'I don't think I'll come to tea if you invite me back,' said Mrs Kennedy. 'I couldn't sit in a beanbag – or even on a coffee table. And what about you, Jake?'

'Oh, I can sit on a coffee table,' said Jake. He'd just located the source of the rose smell. It was a large blue-and-white bowl, big enough to bathe a baby in, half filled with dried rose petals.

'No, I mean, what's your house like?'

'Ordinary,' said Jake. 'It has, you know, furniture. It's not as bad as Stella's, but it's not as good as this.'

'Ah, the golden mean,' said Mrs Kennedy, nodding.

'Are the pictures yours?' Jake asked.

'Most of them,' she said.

'And they let you hang them up?' said Stella.

'They're lucky to have them,' said Mrs Kennedy with a sniff. 'I used to live in my own apartment, but my son thinks I can't look after myself, so he moved me in here – and then he went off on his holidays! I like it here, I'm not complaining, but I'm not used to stairs. I have a terrible job remembering to bring everything down in the mornings, so I won't have to go back up again later in the day, but I always forget, so I do have to go back up. Which reminds me, Jake. Would you run up and get my handbag for me? It's on the chair in the back bedroom. It has my artificial sweetener in it, and I can't take tea without it.'

'Could you not just take sugar?' asked Stella.

'Not allowed,' said Mrs Kennedy. 'Diabetic.'

'Oh!' said Stella. 'I thought you were just slimming.'

Mrs Kennedy laughed. 'Old people have different problems from the young,' she said.

Jake took the stairs two by two. The beautiful young girl watched him all the way, and he watched her. The stair wall was covered in paintings as well, but he didn't stop to examine them. He was too interested in the girl with the candlestick.

'I know someone with diabetes and she's only seven,' Stella was saying when he returned with the handbag.

'Different kind,' said Mrs Kennedy.

Women! Jake thought. Always discussing illnesses.

'Now, I did ask you to tea, but you'll have to make it yourselves. I need to just sit here for a little while and recover. The kettle's boiled, the tray's set, it's all in the kitchen. And the tea is in a caddy by the tray. Indian, I take it?'

'What?' asked Jake.

'Indian tea,' said Mrs Kennedy. 'I imagine that's what you like. Children don't seem to like China.'

'I've got nothing against China,' said Jake, puzzled. 'But I'm sure whatever tea you have is fine.'

'And there's cake, of course,' said Mrs Kennedy. 'Two kinds. Battenberg and porter.'

Jake shrugged. Stella was yanking her head

furiously at him, encouraging him to *come on* –
she was obviously dying to see the kitchen.

'Battenberg and *porter*,' giggled Stella as they went
down the hall to the kitchen. 'It sounds like the army
or something. The captain and his manservant.
"Bring me my gaiters, Porter!" Would you think she
was in the army? Gaiters is a nice word, I think, but
it's not beautiful enough for the wall of honour.'

'Don't be silly,' said Jake. 'There were no women
in the army in her day.'

'Were there not? How do you know?'

'I know a lot, I keep telling you. I read stuff.'

'Look at this!' said Stella excitedly, pointing at
an extraordinary wooden construction, heavily
carved. 'It's Indian. Where the tea comes from,
though I'd say that's a coincidence. There's one
for sale in the Oxfam shop, but it costs a fortune.
It's the only thing in the whole Oxfam shop that
costs a fortune. Isn't it beautiful? There's a pearly
bit here, look.'

'Mother-of-pearl,' Jake said.

'Is that a swear word?' asked Stella.

'No, it's what you call that pearly bit. It's the
lining of oyster shells.'

Jake looked behind the screen, which stood in
front of the space under the stairs. Behind it were
coats and umbrellas and the kinds of things you
expect to find under the stairs, but they were
obviously a bit too untidy for the Kennedys so

they'd put this wooden screen up to conceal them.

'Come on,' he said. 'She'll be wondering what's keeping us.'

He opened the door into the kitchen, and an extraordinary smell hit his nostrils. Fruit and spices and toffee and butter and olives and sugar and wine and marzipan and lemon and tea.

He breathed in. 'Smells glorious,' he said to Stella, who was behind him. She rested her chin on his shoulder and took a deep breath of the kitchen aroma.

'Oh!' she said. 'Maple syrup, roses, mmm, apples.' She sniffed again. 'Rum, cinnamon, raisins, nutmeg. Our kitchen always smells of onions and raw meat.'

Jake didn't say anything to that, because it was roughly true. Though sometimes it smelt of worse things.

Even in the kitchen there was a rug, but only one, in the centre of the flagged floor. A huge scrubbed table stood on the rug, and the chairs around it had deep seats that seemed to be upholstered in a sort of carpet, with thick brass studs. There were pictures here too, in frames, but they were all drawings and cartoons.

'It's King Arthur's kitchen,' said Stella, pointing at a big deer's head looming out of the wall, as if the deer had stuck his great antlered head in for a look.

'His table was round,' said Jake.

'Oh, that was just his business table. His kitchen table was probably rectangular. Though it might be the table of the High King of Ireland at . . . where was it?'

'Tara,' Jake said. 'Ta-ra-ra boom-de-ay, I am the king today!'

He switched on the kettle to bring it back to the boil.

'Oh, look, that's Battenberg cake, isn't it?' he said, pointing at a plate of coloured slices. 'The one with the harlequin squares?'

'Oh yes, and the marzipan icing. It's the brightest yellow I ever saw in a food. I bet it's full of E-numbers. Yippee! We're going to have a feast! Hi-cockalorum, cockalee!'

'Egg yolks are that colour,' said Jake. 'I like her.'

'I like her too,' said Stella.

'No, I mean, I *really* like her,' said Jake. 'She's special.'

'Yeah,' said Stella. 'Sure.'

'Were you in India yourself?' Stella asked, when they got back up to the drawing room with the tea tray.

'No,' said Mrs Kennedy. 'I've never been further east than Hull. Except for two weekends in Paris. And once I went on a day trip to Amsterdam. Can you imagine? Eighteen hours in Holland.'

'Hull? That sounds terribly . . . *dull*!' said Stella

with a sudden screech of laughter at her rhyme. 'Maybe I will be a poet after all, Jake,' she added.

'Oh, it's not dull,' said Mrs Kennedy. 'No place is dull when you get to know what's going on in people's lives.'

'And do you do that?' Stella asked her. 'Get to know what's happening in people's lives?'

'I seem to have the knack,' said Mrs Kennedy. 'And now I'll have a piece of that porter cake, if you don't mind, young Stella.'

'I don't think so,' said Stella. 'You're supposed to be diabetic.'

'I'll only have a small piece,' said Mrs Kennedy. 'Just a nibble.'

27

In a dream that night, Jake thought, 'Poor Daisy, only got one dad.'

Next morning he remembered the dream thought.

What rubbish!

He didn't have two dads. He had half a dad at best. The one who'd run away didn't count, and the one he'd got wasn't the real thing.

28

'So tell me about this stickleback,' said Jake's dad. They were washing up together after dinner. This was a new rule in their house, to give Mum time to feed Daisy in peace. Quite a lot of things had changed since Daisy had arrived.

'What stickleback?' asked Jake, though he knew exactly what Dad meant. He remembered the conversation they'd had a few weeks ago. It seemed a lifetime ago now. He was just playing for time, trying to decide what Dad was getting at.

'The one that goes blue in the face. Like me, trying to talk to you.' Dad coughed a nervous little laugh.

'It goes *red* in the face,' Jake said, 'and blue in the body. Some books say the body has a bluish tinge; others say it goes brilliant blue. I suppose there must be differences between the species. There are lots of species, ones with three spines, ones with ten spines, and I suppose some with the numbers in between. And the eyes go bright, bright blue too, electric blue.'

'Three spines! *Ten* spines! You'd be crippled if you had ten spines. You couldn't walk – or swim.'

'Not that kind of spine,' said Jake, suppressing a sigh. There was no doubt about it, his dad was slow on the uptake. 'It means a little sticky-up bit, a stickle, on the back. Like a thorn on a rose. They're a sort of armour, and weapons too. They get very fierce when they have babies.'

'Oh. So they take fatherhood very seriously, do they, these sticklebacks?'

'Yep,' said Jake, letting the water spill slowly out of the washing-up basin into the sink. The water was pale grey and greasy. He was going to have to wash the basin, to get the film of grease off it. He hunkered down to get the detergent from the press under the sink.

'Well, go on,' said Dad. 'I'm all ears.'

Jake laughed. It was a family joke, because it was true that Dad had rather large ears. Not like Jake's, which, thankfully, were small and lay back neatly against the side of his head. He had his mother's ears. His mother often said so. He didn't know what his father's ears had been like. It wasn't the kind of question you asked your mother, somehow.

'I hope Daisy doesn't inherit your ears,' Jake said, standing up with the squeezy detergent bottle in his hand. 'You should have thought about that before you had her.'

'What! Not have a baby in case her ears stick

out! I don't think that's very sensible, Jake, now, is it?'

Dad was riled, Jake could see. He smiled to himself and rubbed the detergent cream around the inside of the basin.

'But go on about the stickleback,' Dad said. 'I want to know.'

'Well,' said Jake. 'He builds this nest, see? And then he entices the female sticklebacks into it. They are brown, like female ducks, dull, but in the mating season, he is all in his bridal colours. That's what they call it, don't laugh, I'm just telling you.'

'I'm not laughing,' said Dad. 'I'm listening.'

'He does this zigzag dance, it's called a courtship dance, and she watches, and if she likes it, and she likes him and all his colours, and she likes his nest, then she goes in and lays her eggs, and then she swims off.'

'The hussy!'

'Yeah, well. So, he keeps on doing this, getting all the females he can to lay eggs in his nest, and he fertilizes all the eggs of course, so they're all his, genetically – that's the whole point, you see, he *wants* them to have sticky-out ears, you could say. And then he looks after the eggs and he fights off all the predators and, like I said, he is terribly fierce. And even after they hatch out, he looks after them until they are fully independent and able to mind themselves.'

'My word! So that's the difference between sticklebacks and humans, then.'

'Yes, they're better fathers.'

'No, I mean, in humans, it's the female who wears the bridal dress. And all because she wants to pass on her lovely pearly conch-like ears to her offspring, but of course, she doesn't know that's why she's doing it.'

'That's not it at all,' said Jake. 'That's not the point.'

'Well, it's *one* point, Jake,' said Dad. 'And another point is that sticklebacks are interesting *because* they're so unusual. They're not some sort of good example for the rest of the species of the planet, you know. It's just one little corner of evolution, the stickleback school of child maintenance and education.'

Jake didn't know what Dad was on about; but he knew he didn't want to continue this conversation. He felt it was getting all twisted.

'So that's your bedtime story for tonight,' he said, turning the basin upside down in the sink to let it drain.

'Speaking of bridal dress,' Dad went on, 'you know there's going to be a christening soon?'

Jake hadn't known, but he nodded anyway.

'So we thought . . . your mum and I . . . we thought . . .'

Jake kept his eyes glued to the upturned bottom

of the washing-up basin. He couldn't look at Dad.

'We thought, Jake, that we might get married, make one big celebration of it. What do you think, son?'

'*What!*' Jake spun around from the sink to face his dad.

'Well, you know, we are a family, after all. And we're planning to stay being a family. Wouldn't it be nice, Jake, to sort of *announce* it?'

'But then, everyone will know you weren't married to start with.'

'So?'

'Well . . . I don't know, it feels peculiar. Then you'd be my stepfather.'

'I am already.'

'But legally.'

'I don't think it makes much difference, legally. You're still Jim's son, from the strictly stickleback point of view, if you see what I mean, and your ears will never stick out quite as well as mine do . . .' He stopped here for Jake to laugh and, in spite of himself, Jake did give a small smile. 'But I've been your dad for as long as you can remember, Jake. It doesn't matter who's married to whom.'

'If it doesn't matter,' Jake said, 'why bother?'

'It doesn't matter to you and me, I mean,' Dad said. 'It matters in other ways. Your mother and I would like to be married.'

'Because of Daisy.'

'Not only because of Daisy, Jake.'

'It didn't matter when it was just me.'

'Jake, I know it must seem like that.'

'Because it *is* like that.'

'No!' said Dad. 'We always intended doing it, but, well, we just let it drift . . . and then Daisy coming along just sort of *reminded* us.'

Jake stared at him, a long, cold stare. Dad stared back. He looked very uncomfortable, but he kept staring anyway, as if willing Jake to agree.

'Oh, do what you like,' said Jake at last. 'What does it matter anyway? I don't care what you do.'

29

The weather had improved dramatically, which was lucky because they were having the wedding-cum-christening in the garden. At least, they had the actually getting married and getting christened part in the local church, and then they had the party in the garden, in the sunshine.

It all happened very fast. Jake hardly had time to think about it.

'So that's the proof, Father,' Jake's mum was saying to the priest who'd done the marrying and christening, as she served him his wedding lunch. 'Salmon and raspberries just couldn't be in season at the same time by a quirk of evolution, it's too *divine* a coincidence.'

'So that means there's a God?' said the priest, looking startled.

'Mmm,' said Jake's mum, grinning at him.

'Well, it's not a proof known to theology,' the priest said, 'but it's pretty convincing, I must say.'

'You could write a paper on it in a theological

journal and send it to the Vatican and they might make you a bishop,' Jake's mum suggested, waving her fish slice in the air. 'I'd never let on I told you. It'd be our little secret. Have some more champagne.'

'So does this mean we'll be seeing more of you at Mass?' the priest asked slyly.

'Oh, now!' said Jake's mum non-committally. 'You never know your luck.'

'You're drunk,' Jake hissed at her as the priest moved off with his plate of salmon and his glass of champagne, chuckling to himself.

'Only the teeniest bit, Jakey,' she said.

Her eyes were shining. She looked lovely, in her pearly-coloured dress and with her hair all caught into a flowery headdress, though it had begun to work itself a bit loose by now and was drifting around her head in its usual wild way.

'It's not every day you get married,' Jake's mother was saying. 'And champagne doesn't make you drunk, you know. It only makes you merry. Have a Coke, why don't you, Jake?'

'I'm full of bubbles already, thanks,' Jake said. 'And I know when I've had enough. I hope Daisy doesn't get drunk. Can you imagine, a baby with a hangover? Ugh!'

'Jake, I've only had two glasses. Stop lecturing me. It's my wedding day!'

Jake shrugged. 'I hope you don't think I'm going to change my name,' he said.

'What?' asked his mother. 'Why would you change your name?'

'Well, boys usually have the same name as their fathers. Isn't that why people get married?'

'Or their mothers, Jake, as you have had all your life.'

'But you will be changing your name now. "Mrs Burke." Ugh! It sounds so *old*, Mum.'

'You just think that because it's your granny's name. But anyway, I have no intention of changing my name, Jake. It's not obligatory, you know, and I haven't a notion of it, so you see, there is no problem.'

'So you and I will still be Cotter?'

'Of course.'

'And Dad will still be Burke?'

'Yes.'

'And what about Daisy?'

'I don't know. I hadn't thought about it. Burke, I suppose.'

'You see! It's different for her. Because of your stupid wedding. That's why you did it, so she could be a proper Burke.'

'Jake, this is ridiculous. Can we have this conversation some other time, some other place?'

'No,' said Jake. 'I think this is a good time.'

'You can be Burke too if you like, darling, if you want to be the same as Daisy. I'm sure you can fill in a form or something. It's no big deal and we can discuss it *another time*, Jake.'

'I just told you, Mum, I *don't want to* change my name.'

'All right then! Don't!' his mother yelled at him. 'That's just what I've been saying all along. You *don't have to*! There IS no *issue*, Jake.'

Jake's mother never yelled at him, but now she was shouting and her two fists were clenched in the air in front of her, and she was rocking back and forth, as if she wanted to shake him. He was so startled he let out a loud gasp and burst into tears. It was the shock, more than anything, of seeing his mother so exasperated with him. They never fought. And he never cried.

'Jake, Jake, I'm sorry!' His mother hunkered down with the crinkling sound of her wedding dress folding around her as she sank, and opened her arms to him.

He longed to run into those outstretched arms and hug her, but something made him hang back. Maybe it was stubbornness, or maybe it was embarrassment at his own tears, or maybe it was just the thought of the starchy texture of her dress crunching against his face. But he stood there and shook his head, and fought to push back the tears.

30

Jake was invited to Stella's for tea on the day after the wedding. He was glad to get away. His parents had announced that morning that they were on their honeymoon, and they had no intention of doing anything for the whole weekend except staying late in bed reading the papers, and watching some crime thing on the television. Jake was to help himself to leftovers from the wedding party and not interrupt. His mother would have to feed Daisy, of course, but that was the only thing they were definitely doing all day.

The kitchen was in chaos. No wonder his parents didn't want to get up and face it. Jake found the cornflakes easily, but he had to wash a cereal bowl that someone had clearly eaten raspberry pavlova out of. He scrubbed the bowl hard and tried not to think about the person who'd last eaten out of it, but his heart wasn't in it, and he only ate half the cornflakes.

When Stella rang to invite him to tea, he was

thrilled to accept. He told his stunned parents that he expected to see some order in the kitchen by the time he got home, and left early, because he'd decided that he would visit Mrs Kennedy before presenting himself at Stella's.

Mrs Kennedy was surprised to see him. She hadn't heard about the wedding.

'That's nice,' she said, when Jake told her the story. 'You must be pleased.'

'Why?' asked Jake. 'What's it got to do with me?'

'Well, I don't know, but you must be pleased for your mother.'

'I'm not,' said Jake. It felt good to be able to tell someone this, someone who wasn't going to get upset about it.

'And it must be nice to know that your dad is, you know, legally your stepfather.'

'Not really,' said Jake.

'Do you feel bad about your other father?' Mrs Kennedy asked. 'Is that the problem? Do you miss him?'

'No,' said Jake. 'I don't miss him, exactly. But I wish he hadn't just disappeared. It's not a nice feeling to think that a person left because you were born.'

'Oh, I'm sure that wasn't the reason.'

'I think so,' said Jake. 'That's more or less how Mum explained it, anyway.'

'Oh, well,' said Mrs Kennedy, 'all families are different, aren't they?'

'No,' said Jake. 'Most families are the same. Anyway, I don't want to talk about families.'

'You're right,' said Mrs Kennedy. 'Very dull.'

'Like Hull,' said Jake.

'Not in the slightest,' said Mrs Kennedy. 'I'll tell you what. I have something to show you, only you'll have to get it yourself.'

'OK,' said Jake.

'You know where my room is, don't you? Well, go into the room beside that, it's the study, if you don't mind.'

'We have a study,' said Jake. 'My mother works there.'

'Well, my daughter-in-law does nothing at all. Anyway, there is a thing in there called library steps. Do you know what those are?'

'Yes,' said Jake. 'Like a little ladder.'

'That's it. Now, take this little ladder thing and go into my room, and climb up to the top of the wardrobe.'

Jake laughed.

'No, I mean, just so you can *see* the top of the wardrobe.'

'All right,' said Jake.

'You will see a hatbox there. It's a pink-and-white-striped cylinder. Behind the hatbox is a shoebox. That's the thing I want.'

'All right,' said Jake again, wondering what could be in the shoebox. Jewels maybe. Or money.

He went up the stairs, past all the paintings. He winked at the beautiful girl with the candle.

Or a letter from a famous person to another famous person, he thought. Like from Napoleon to Florence Nightingale. Or a will. Or bomb-making equipment. Or the title deeds to a castle in Transylvania. Or the plans of a dungeon where Mrs Kennedy's ancestors were buried. Or a skull.

He found the library steps. He climbed up to the wardrobe. He sneezed. He moved the pink-and-white hatbox to one side and sneezed again. It was very dusty on top of the wardrobe. He found the shoebox, white with black writing on it.

Carefully he lifted it down and put it on the bed. Then he returned the library steps to the study, and went back into the bedroom for the shoebox.

It couldn't be anything alive, he thought, because it would die of hunger and thirst and lack of air in the shoebox. But it might be an egg. A dragon's egg. Or an ostrich egg. On the whole, an ostrich egg was more likely. It felt a bit heavy for an egg, even a big one, but he held it carefully all the same and carried it downstairs.

'Why do you keep it on top of the wardrobe?' he asked as he came back into the sitting room. 'You must have an awful job getting it down.'

'To keep it safe,' said Mrs Kennedy. 'I can get it down easily enough by poking at it with my stick.

A stick has many purposes, you know, apart from holding you up when you get wobbly on your feet. Also, I'm taller than you.'

Jake thought it must be something pretty precious if she put it away so carefully.

'Postcards!' he said, when she took the lid off.

'Yes,' she said. 'Lovely ones.'

'Oh!' said Jake.

'You sound disappointed,' said Mrs Kennedy. 'Are postcards not exciting enough for you?'

'No,' said Jake. All this honesty was going to his head.

'Oh, they're not holiday ones,' said Mrs Kennedy. 'They're ones of paintings.'

That sounded marginally better, but not as good as the castle in Transylvania or the dragon's egg.

'But the house is full of real paintings. Why would you want postcards of paintings?'

'To send to my friends,' she replied.

'Like the one you sent me,' he said, slightly shamefaced at his lack of enthusiasm. 'But even so . . .' he said.

'The thing is, the paintings in the house are all ones I have bought over the years, and I love them all, but I don't have any truly great paintings, by the Old Masters. They cost thousands. Millions. You only get to see them in art galleries, and then you buy a few postcards of them as a souvenir. Like a consolation prize.'

'I've never been to an art gallery,' Jake said. 'I thought they'd be boring.'

'Like Hull?' said Mrs Kennedy. 'Well, they are like Hull – not as dull as you'd expect, as long as you are prepared to look hard. And if you want to be a fish painter, I'd say you should go and look at a few fish paintings, don't you think?'

'Are there others? Apart from the one you sent?'

'Of course. Oodles.'

'You mean, lots of other people have painted fish?' asked Jake, surprised.

'Yes,' said Mrs Kennedy. 'Come on, I'll show you.'

It was the strangest thing. Mrs Kennedy had a whole shoebox full of fish paintings. Jake was in heaven. Well, actually, there were a few other things as well in the paintings. Not absolutely every one had fish. Some had dead pheasants. Some just had apples and pears. Some had a Bible and a globe and a tablecloth. Some just had a group of jugs. But they were all pictures of things on tables.

'But do you know something queer?' Mrs Kennedy said, as they examined the postcards. 'People don't like pictures of dead fish. They must give them the creeps, or something. The thing is, if you have a picture of, say, grapes or watermelons or something like that, and let's say it's by an important painter, and it's worth, oh, let's say half a million euro – it's mostly dead painters whose paintings are that expensive, by the way – well now, if you have a picture by the same artist only it's of a dead fish, it's probably worth only about half that. Isn't that the oddest thing?'

'Why?'

'Well, people don't like looking at dead things, I suppose. They don't want to have them on their walls. So the paintings aren't as valuable.'

'Does this mean I shouldn't be a fish painter?' asked Jake.

'Well, it means you should probably only paint live fish.'

'But you couldn't do that,' Jake protested. 'They wouldn't keep still long enough.'

'That's a point. Maybe you could photograph them instead. Or film them. You could be a fish filmer.'

'Is there such a thing?' asked Jake.

'There must be,' said Mrs Kennedy, 'because you do see fish on the television, from time to time, don't you?'

'I suppose,' said Jake. 'And they are usually wiffling, aren't they? Which means they're alive.'

'I wouldn't know,' said Mrs Kennedy. 'I don't think I've heard of wiffling.'

'It's Stella's word. She probably made it up. She's good with words. I think she should be a poet when she grows up.'

'There's no money in poetry,' said Mrs Kennedy. 'Even less than in fish painting, I'd say.'

'Oh, well,' said Jake, 'I suppose we could work in McDonald's for our real jobs and only paint fish and write poems at the weekends. Do you think that would work?'

'Possibly,' said Mrs Kennedy.

31

'Where've you been?' asked Stella, opening the door to him. 'I said four o'clock.'

'Having lunch with Mrs Kennedy,' said Jake.

'Lunch? But it's after five.'

'Well, it was a late lunch,' Jake explained. 'And then I helped her with the washing up, and that took ages, because she does everything so slowly, and then . . .'

'What did you have for lunch?' asked Stella.

'Tomato sandwiches and cold sausages and frozen peas, only we unfroze them, of course. And then we were still hungry so we fried some eggs. And we finished the porter cake from last week.'

'She isn't supposed to eat cake,' said Stella.

'No,' said Jake. 'But she does. She does what she likes. She says it's the only advantage of being old. There's no one else who's old enough to be able to tell you not to. Her son tells her what to do, she says, but she doesn't listen to him, because after all, she's changed his nappy.'

'Oh, yuck,' said Stella.

'I thought you liked babies,' said Jake.

'That's not the point,' said Stella.

'Do you think your mum or dad could show me how to photograph fish?' Jake asked.

'No,' said Stella sulkily.

'Why not?'

'Because they work in a studio. They don't have underwater cameras. They're not Jacques Cousteau, you know.'

'No, but they might be able to . . .'

'Oh, Jake, give it over,' said Stella. 'I invite you here and you've been wuffling on about Mrs Kennedy and porter cake and underwater photography since you arrived, and I don't want to talk about those things. I want you to help me to cook.'

'Cook?' said Jake doubtfully. 'I thought you'd invited me to tea. "Wuffling"'s a good word, by the way,' he added, seeing a frown forming between her eyebrows. 'Is it related to "wiffling"?'

'I don't know,' said Stella. 'I haven't decided. I did invite you to tea, but I didn't think you'd mind helping with the cooking. Will you be able to eat it after all that lunch?'

'No problem,' said Jake.

'OK,' said Stella, cheering up. 'Right, you can chop the onions. We're having spaghetti.'

32

Stella's parents were doing a jigsaw with Joanne, Stella's littlest sister, at the kitchen table. There were three children under the table – they seemed to like sitting under tables – two of them banging upside-down saucepans with wooden spoons, but nobody seemed to mind the noise, except Jake. Another child was sitting at the other end of the table, doing sums, or so it appeared.

Joanne looked up.

'Dake!' she said and opened and closed her hand at him.

That was supposed to be a wave, Jake conjectured, and he waved back.

Stella's mother looked around. 'Ah, Jake,' she said with a grin. 'The Pied Piper of Mount Gregor.'

'What?' said Jake.

'You know, the one who spirits children away? The Pied Piper. I hear you took all my daughters fishing. Not a clever move, Jake, if you don't mind my saying so.'

'I never . . .'

'Yes, you did, Jake,' said Stella resolutely. 'It was your idea to go fishing, wasn't it?'

'Yes, but . . .'

'However, we forgive you,' said Stella's dad, 'because we heard you tried to rescue one of them. Which one we aren't quite sure.' He finished with a short laugh that sounded like he didn't really think it was all that funny.

'How do you do?' said Jake firmly. He was going to be polite even if they weren't. He'd never met this person before, and that was the right thing to say in the circumstances. 'I really did rescue a little girl,' he added defensively.

'How do you do?' answered Stella's dad, looking slightly embarrassed at his own rudeness. 'Name's Brian. This is Rosie.' He nodded towards Stella's mum. 'But it wasn't our little girl that you rescued.'

'No, but it might have been,' said Jake stoutly.

'Precisely my point,' said Brian. 'Any one of them might have fallen in and drowned. I don't think it was very responsible of you to take them all fishing with you, that's all. They're very young. But, as I say, we have forgiven you, so let's forget about it.'

'But . . .' Jake was seething. He looked at Stella for support, but Stella was mouthing and making wild gestures that he couldn't interpret, except for the last one, where she drew her finger dramatically across her throat. He got the message, and shut up.

'Edel is just working out how much spaghetti we will need,' Stella's mum explained, when she noticed Jake looking curiously at the girl doing the sums.

'Yes,' said Brian. 'She's been having a spot of bother in the maths department, don't you know, so we get her to do all the kitchen sums, just for practice.'

'But does she not get them wrong?' Jake asked in a whisper, so as not to insult Edel.

'Usually,' said Stella's dad. 'But she's getting better at working out how it goes. The actual answer is not the important part.'

'Except that you do need the correct answer if it has to do with how much food to cook,' said Jake practically.

'Not really,' said Brian. 'If she gets it wrong by too much, we have leftovers. And if she gets it wrong by too little, we just fill up on bread and butter. The main thing is the working out.'

'Two and a half kilos,' announced Edel.

'I don't think so, Dell,' said her dad kindly. 'Have another go. Not even this lot could eat two and a half kilos of spaghetti. I mean, I wouldn't mind letting them try, but we haven't got a pot big enough to cook it in.'

Edel scrunched up her forehead and went on calculating.

'Half a kilo,' she said in a moment.

Brian went to the kitchen press and took out a packet of spaghetti. 'This is half a kilo, Edel,' he said. Then he took out four more packets. 'And all together, this is two and a half kilos.'

She stared, nodded, and stared again.

'Now, Edel, do you think we could eat five whole packets of spaghetti for one meal?'

'No,' she said.

'Right, so your first answer had to be wrong. Now, what about a single packet? Do you think that would be enough? For all of us? Count Jake in too.'

'No,' she said again.

'So what is the right answer to the sum?' Brian asked.

Edel looked at her piece of paper.

She looked at the packets of spaghetti.

'Two packets,' she announced.

'That's more like it,' said her dad, and put three packets back in the press.

'But she hasn't done the sum,' said Jake. 'She's just guessed.'

'True,' said Brian. 'But it was an intelligent guess. That's a start.'

Jake shook his head. He thought two packets was probably still too much, but he didn't argue.

'Help me with the onions, Jake,' Stella commanded.

It was true about their kitchen smelling of onions and raw meat. Today at any rate.

'Huh-way!' screeched Joanne suddenly. 'Huh-way!'

Jake looked up from his onion-chopping. Joanne had finished her jigsaw, it seemed, and was having a little celebration. She clapped her hands and cried, 'Huh-way!' again.

'Good for you, Joey!' he said, and she beamed at him.

When the onions were chopped, Stella said it was time to set the table.

'But the jigsaw!' objected Jake. 'What about Joanne's jigsaw?'

Joanne spread her hands out over it protectively.

'Easy,' said Rosie, taking a thick blanket out of a drawer. 'Help me to spread this out, Jake. We just need to lower it gently over the table, so as not to disturb the jigsaw.'

The children under the table whooped with feigned terror as the blanket was lowered over the table and settled over the sides, darkening their under-table den. They banged their saucepans extra hard and laughed loudly. Jake would have covered his ears against the noise if he hadn't been holding one end of the blanket.

After Stella's mother had smoothed out the blanket very carefully, Jake helped her to spread a bright-red check tablecloth over the blanket.

'Now, set the table, please, Jake,' said Rosie. 'Cutlery is in that drawer there. Joanne will help you, won't you, Joey?'

Jake had never been ordered about like this in anyone else's house, but he did as he was told and he handed spoons to Joanne, as he didn't think knives or forks would be the safest thing for her. She carried the spoons one at a time from the drawer to the table.

A head appeared from under the tablecloth as Jake was laying out the cutlery.

'Hi, Jake,' said the head.

He could feel its breath on his knee.

'Hi,' he answered, squinting down. He didn't know which sister it belonged to.

The youngest one, the little boy, crawled out from under the table and sat on the floor. He started to try to unbuckle Jake's sandals as he stood at the table.

The head laughed.

'Stoppit!' said Jake, and shook his foot.

Rosie glared at Jake and scooped the child up.

'Come on, Fergie,' she said. 'Let's get you into your high chair, where you'll be safe.'

'Sorry,' muttered Jake. 'I'm not used to so many children.'

'Why not?' asked Rosie. 'Do you not go to school?'

'Yeah,' said Jake dejectedly. 'I do.'

She'd got him there.

33

'You abandoned me!' Jake hissed at Stella when they were finally alone together, a couple of hours later, in the back garden.

They'd all eaten and then there'd been an interminable amount of washing up, even though Stella's family had a dishwasher, because there were so many odd-shaped things that didn't fit in the machine.

'I never did,' said Stella. 'I was there every minute.'

'No, I mean you let me take the blame for the fishing.'

'Well, it was your idea, Jake, you have to admit that.'

'But I didn't want all your sisters there! That wasn't part of the plan.'

'And what was I supposed to do with them? Tie them to their beds and leave little bowls of water for them?'

'I don't know,' said Jake. 'But it had nothing to do with me. I didn't *like* the idea of their being there, you may remember. I was nervous.'

'I see,' said Stella stiffly. 'You have a problem with me having a lot of sisters, is that it? Well, I'm sorry, that's just how it is. I can't send them back. There isn't some sort of return counter for unwanted siblings, you know.'

She turned away from him and started to climb the cherry tree.

'I *know* that,' said Jake to her back. Boy, did he know it! But he couldn't work out how he'd got into this argument. It didn't seem to be going the way he'd expected. He didn't know what to say next. All he knew was that he was being wronged. And Stella was the one doing it. 'But it's not fair,' he added. He could hear the whine in his voice. He didn't like it, but he couldn't help himself.

Stella didn't say anything.

'I'd better go home,' he said heavily, almost to himself.

'Yes, maybe you'd better,' said Stella. She'd evidently heard him, even though he thought he'd spoken very quietly.

She didn't say goodbye. She didn't even look around at him. She just went on climbing the cherry tree.

Jake felt as if there was a stone in his chest. It did sound whiny to say it wasn't fair, but it was true; it wasn't. He hadn't said anything about Stella having too many sisters. He'd only said he hadn't liked taking them all fishing. And now it seemed he was somehow in trouble with Stella's parents for doing the very thing he hadn't wanted to do, and *hadn't* actually done. It was Stella who had done it. He wanted to shout at her, but instead he just breathed very hard and stomped to the back door, dashed through the house before anyone saw him, and slipped quietly out the front door.

All the way home, the words 'It's not fair!' kept ringing in his head.

He kicked a stone in the gutter, but it was too heavy to roll away and now his toe hurt.

He wasn't going back to Stella's, he decided, as he limped in his garden gate. Not unless she apologized.

34

Jake's parents had got one of those slings for carrying Daisy around in. His mum thought it might be a good idea for Jake to try it on too.

Jake knew what this was about. It was about trying to make him take more of an interest in Daisy.

She had a point.

So he let his mother slip the sling on over his shoulders and click it into place behind his back, and he watched as she then slid one side of it down off his shoulder, to make space for the baby; very carefully she worked Daisy's little body in between the fabric of the sling and Jake's chest, poked her chubby little legs into the legholes, and then raised the shoulder strap of the sling again, and pulled it tight, so that Daisy was snuggled safely against her brother's chest.

He tried to look at her, but all he could see was the top of her downy, bald head, her scalp showing pinkly through her lick of pale, fair hair.

She was heavier than he expected, and he had to make a bow with his arms under her body to support her weight. He could feel her breath hot and damp against his breastbone, and her fast little heartbeat pittered away against his ribs, through his Manchester United top.

'OK, now, walk,' his mother commanded, and Jake gingerly took a few steps across the kitchen floor.

'Are your shoulders aching?' she asked him.

'No,' he said bravely, though they were, 'but she kicks.'

'She's just exercising her little legs,' his mother said dotingly.

'Right,' said Jake as she dunted him again in the thighs.

'OK, I'll take her now,' said his mother anxiously. 'I don't want to tire you out.'

But Jake knew she really didn't trust him to hold the baby carefully enough.

He stood still as she slid the strap over his shoulder again, and pulled Daisy away from him.

Daisy yelled and yelled as her feet kicked free of the legholes of the sling. Jake undid the strap at the back and slithered out of the sling, and then quickly put his hands over his ears. Daisy went on yelling and roaring. His mother sang softly to her, and popped her quickly into her rocking chair, to distract her, but the baby went on yelling and waving her arms. She had made little fists of her hands, and she opened and closed them, opened and closed them frantically in the direction of Jake.

'I think she wants me to hold her again,' said Jake wonderingly.

'Oh, you don't need to,' said his mother. 'Hand me that rattle there, we'll soon distract her.'

But Daisy kept on crying. She pushed the rattle out of her mother's hand, and it clattered noisily to the floor, the little beads inside it rattling like crazy.

'Here,' said Jake. 'Give her to me.'

He held out his arms, and his mother reluctantly unstrapped Daisy from her chair and handed her back to Jake.

Instantly the crying stopped. Daisy snuggled and snuffled into Jake's collarbone, and he lightly touched the top of her head. Her body gave a couple of spasmodic sobs, and then she settled, and gave just an occasional little sigh. Jake went on stroking the top of her head with the tips of his fingers. Within moments, the baby was asleep.

'Well!' said his mother. 'And I thought I was the only one who could do that!'

'Oh, it's a family gift,' said Jake, laughing, but very quietly, so as not to wake her.

35

'The Daisy follows soft the Sun,' Jake's mother often whispered as she dressed Daisy or bathed her or fed her.

'You know, I used to be the Sun, Jake,' she said, 'but I think the centre of her universe has changed.'

'How d'you mean?'

'Well, it's you she follows. You are the golden walker, Jake. Watch. Go out the door, and come back in, and see her little face light up.'

'Don't be silly, Mum.'

'Just do it, Jake, I want to show you.'

Jake sighed, but he did as he was told. He stood outside the door for a few moments, to give Daisy the idea that he was good and gone, and then he opened the door again and poked his head in.

Sure enough, Daisy's eyes lit up, and she waved her arms at him and kicked her legs.

Jake laughed.

'"And when his golden walk is done – / Sits

shyly at his feet." See, that's the closest she can get to sitting at your feet.'

'OK,' he said, 'maybe she does like to see me.'

'No doubt about it.'

'But it's just because babies like children. It's a well-known fact.'

'Hmm,' said Jake's mother. 'If you say so, Mr Smarty-Pants Encyclopedia-Eater.'

36

It was Dad's idea to go for that walk, 'just me and my children', he said. He'd taken to talking about 'my children', to give Jake the idea that he considered him and Daisy equally his. This was silly, because Jake didn't mind any more about all that. He'd got over it. But then, of course, how was Dad to know that?

'We'll walk over as far as your friend's house,' he suggested to Jake. 'And then, if your friend is at home, you can give Daisy to me, and I'll skip off home with her, and you can stay and . . . visit your friend, whatever you two do.'

'Her name is Stella.'

'That's the one. The very thin girl. I have an envelope to deliver to a house on that road anyway.'

'I don't really want to,' said Jake.

'But you haven't seen her for ages,' said Dad. 'Have you?'

'No,' said Jake, looking firmly at the ground.

'Had a row?' asked Dad.

'No!' said Jake and shuffled his feet. It hadn't been a row, exactly. You couldn't call it that. It had just been some sort of stupid *thing* that had happened.

'Sounds like one of those nos that mean yes,' said Dad.

Jake shrugged. He wouldn't mind seeing Stella, just by chance, like.

'Well, look, I have to deliver this letter anyway, so why don't you come with me? You don't have to visit Stella if you don't want to.'

Jake shrugged again, but he stood still while Dad hooked him up with Daisy in the sling.

They walked along together in the early evening sunshine, and Jake tried not to think what he would say if he met Stella.

As they rounded the corner into Stella's cul-de-sac, there seemed to be children everywhere. A bunch of girls were playing a skipping game on the pavement at the far end of the road, out of the way of passing cars. Stella didn't seem to be among them, but he recognized a couple of her sisters. A few boys were sitting on a garden wall, not doing anything much, except pushing each other off the wall.

Jake could see Stella's little sister Joanne crouched on the pavement outside their house, poking in the gutter with a long stick. He smiled at the sight of her, and was just about to say to Dad, 'Look, that's

Joanne, otherwise known as Joey,' when he realized his father had slipped into a gateway.

'I'll just be a sec, Jake,' Dad said, waving the envelope. 'Don't drop Daisy.'

'No fear,' said Jake, and fondled his little sister's feet. She squirmed and gurgled.

There was a shiny new car in Stella's driveway, Jake noticed. It was quite small, sky blue, and looked as if it was smiling. It's funny, it occurred to him, how things can happen so quickly; how someone you thought you knew suddenly has a new car, and you had no idea. You wouldn't even know to wave if you saw it beetling by on the road.

Just then, Stella's mother came charging out of the house, a scarlet scarf flying behind her.

Joanne looked up and saw Jake. She hadn't seen him for days. Her face broke into a smile.

'Hey, Joanne!' Jake called to her, and waved.

Rosie yanked open the door of the sky-blue car, got in and banged the door shut. The engine revved up almost immediately.

'Dake!' Joanne shouted back and started to run towards him, her long stick still in one hand.

Jake saw it all.

In – slow – motion.

The little girl running towards him, her arms outstretched, the smiling, sky-blue car backing out of the driveway, the child's face turned towards him, heedless of the car.

He raced towards her, jogging the baby in his arms, screaming at the child to watch out, watch out, WATCH OUT, but his breath came in gasps and he couldn't make himself heard over the engine of the car.

The girls at the end of the road must have heard him, though, and they stopped their skipping to watch.

The car inched forward again and straightened up a little, and Jake's breath escaped in a wild exhalation of relief. Daisy was crying, bewildered by the jogging and the shouting.

The girls laughed and started up the rope again.

'Shh, shh,' Jake said, half-heartedly, to Daisy, but it did nothing to soothe the frantic, frightened baby in his arms.

And then suddenly the car shot backwards again. By now, Jake was almost close enough to yank Joanne out of its path. Four or five more desperate strides and he could grab her out of harm's way.

But he hesitated. He couldn't step into the path of the hurtling car, not with Daisy in his arms. He kept shouting, hoping Rosie would hear him, though she was inside the car with the windows all shut and the engine running. His arms hugged Daisy desperately to his body, as if by holding on to her he could somehow save Joanne.

But Rosie didn't hear him, and the car kept lurching backwards. As Jake stood dithering on the pavement, the shiny back bumper of the pretty car clipped the child sideways on, at speed, and Joanne's little body flew sideways into the air, all flailing limbs, like a cat who has missed its footing in an upwards leap, the long stick whipped out of her hand, turning and turning, like the only visible spoke in an invisible wheel. The little girl seemed almost to float to the ground and landed soundlessly in the middle of the road, like a fallen star, all akimbo, utterly still. The stick rolled away on the camber of the road, into the gutter.

The car stopped short, inches from the fallen child, and the door opened. A screaming woman tumbled out.

The girls with the rope dropped it and came running.

Jake could hear his own screams, but he could not control them. They seemed to come from deep inside his body. He could hear them and feel them as they laboured out of his chest cavity, and he could feel how they reverberated against Daisy. Her screams echoed back at him, high and terrified at this terrible, noisy grief that beat against her body, and all the time, he held her in a grasp of steel.

He screamed in terror. He screamed in anguish, for Joanne, for her mother. And he screamed out of his own guilt. If he had not rounded the corner at just that moment, if he had not called to the child, if she had not been so surprised to see him, if she had only been used to seeing him every day, the way it used to be; if he and Stella, in other words, were not at loggerheads over . . . what? Over nothing . . . If he had not been hampered by the baby in his arms . . .

'Jake!'

His father was shaking his shoulders.

'Jake, stop screeching! What is it? Give me Daisy! You're suffocating her.'

Dad hadn't seen it yet. His whole attention was fixed on his screaming children.

Jake loosened his grip on Daisy and raised his arm to point, though he could hardly hold it steady, and at last Dad saw it – the halted, guilty car, the stricken mother stumbling towards the lifeless body of her child, the little girls standing open-mouthed in a semicircle, the skipping rope lying abandoned like a snake behind them.

'It was the accelerator, it was the accelerator,' Rosie Daly was shouting, over and over, and sobbing. 'I meant to stamp on the brake, the brake, the bra-aa-ake.'

37

On the third morning, another card came for Jake, with another dead fish on it. It was a different picture. This time the fish was peeping out of the top of a canvas bag that was hanging from a peg in what looked like a scullery.

Jake had lain for two days in bed, refusing to get up, except to use the toilet, refusing to eat, refusing to speak to anyone. At night he woke screaming from nightmares that always ended in the same way, with that sickening fall and then the awful stillness and then his own screams. His face was permanently swollen from crying. His throat was raw, his nose peeling and chafed; his eyes were stinging from excess salt. His mother changed his sodden pillow and brought him ice cream as if he were a person with tonsillitis, but he pushed it aside.

He couldn't eat ice cream. He couldn't bear to be himself.

Daisy cried all the time. It was as if she knew there'd been some dreadful catastrophe, but of course it was just the shock. Her mother took her to see Jake, to try to soothe her, and to try to shake Jake out of himself, but he turned to the wall and lay staring at it until she went away, with Daisy whimpering in her arms.

'I'm on my way,' said the card. 'I know you will see me.'

It was signed M squiggle K squiggle, as before.

Jake stared dully at it. There was no stamp, he noticed. She must have delivered it herself, or sent someone with it. Who? Her son, perhaps, the daisy-murderer. That was some joke, he thought bitterly to himself. Who was the murderer now?

'When did it come?' he whispered to his mother, who had brought the card to him.

'I don't know. I found it in the hall just now.'

'I'd better get up,' Jake said, sitting up in bed. His head pounded with the tears he hadn't shed yet.

His mother was visibly startled, but she said nothing.

'I mean, she can't come up the stairs, not very well, she's an old lady with arthritis.' Jake sniffed.

'I see,' said his mother.

'She might come any time,' Jake said.

'I suppose so.'

'I'll have a shower,' Jake said, and swung his feet out of the bed.

'Right,' said his mother. 'And a cup of tea and toast?'

'Battenberg cake,' said Jake. 'She likes Battenberg cake. Or porter cake.'

'No, I mean, for you,' said his mother.

'Oh, yes,' said Jake.

'Right,' said Mum again. 'You go and have that shower, and I'll find some clean clothes for you.'

38

'Stella sent me,' said Mrs Kennedy. 'In a manner of speaking.'

Jake was sitting in the living room, all clean and neat, but feeling hollow inside, as if he were a pillow whose stuffing had been emptied out. Mrs Kennedy was sitting opposite him, her three-legged stick standing by her chair. A plate of Swiss roll slices − not Battenberg, there hadn't been any, Jake's mother had explained breathlessly − sat on the table between them, with two cups of milky tea.

Jake said nothing. It wasn't that he didn't want to. It was that he didn't trust himself not to cry if he opened his mouth.

'She wants you to come to the funeral,' said Mrs Kennedy. 'That is to say, she needs you there.'

Jake said, 'Did she tell you that?' His voice was cracked, and it hurt to talk.

'Not in so many words, but I know she does. It's tomorrow, eleven o'clock. Can you come, Jake?'

Jake shook his head. He couldn't possibly go. He couldn't bear to see the little coffin, the weeping family, Stella distraught. What could he say to her? He couldn't tell her he was sorry for saying . . . what had he said, anyway? He hadn't said he didn't like her sisters being around, he was sure he hadn't. He definitely hadn't said she had too many sisters. She'd just chosen to interpret it that way.

'Jake, you've had a dreadful shock.'

Jake nodded.

'But it wasn't your fault.'

'It was,' he said listlessly. 'Partly.'

'Do you remember the last card I sent you?'

Jake nodded again. His mouth felt dry. He took a sip of his tea.

'That was because you had saved a child's life. Remember?'

He nodded miserably.

'So, would you think that a boy who did that would have let another child get killed if he could help it?'

'No,' said Jake. 'But . . .'

If he'd run faster, Jake knew, he just *knew*, he could have scooped Joanne up and twirled them all three out of danger. If only he could have run a little faster! If only he hadn't stopped to think! If only he'd done as he did that day at the pier, and acted on instinct! He could have stood out of the path of the car and pulled her towards him. He could have pounded on the roof of the car and forced the driver to stop.

'But me no buts,' said Mrs Kennedy. 'It's as plain as the nose on your face.'

'It *was* my fault,' he said. 'I called to her. I waved to her. She didn't see the car because she was running to *me*.'

'Jake, listen. You are just not that important, you know.'

Jake stared at her.

'But it was my fault,' he whispered. She didn't understand.

'You are not important, *at all*.'

Jake had no idea what she meant. He put his head in his hands.

'Listen,' she said. 'A little girl has died in a tragic accident. As if that is not bad enough, her poor mother was driving the car that killed her.'

Jake gasped, as if someone had hit him with a fistful of nettles.

'But it was . . .'

'Stop! And think. Who is important here, Jake? A boy who happened, by chance, to be on the street and by coincidence was the unwitting cause of the little girl's distraction? A boy who could not prevent the accident because, if he had tried, his own little sister might have been killed also, not to mention himself. Is the boy the important one, or is it the mother of the dead child, who killed her little daughter by accident?'

'The mother,' whispered Jake.

'And how important is the boy?'

'Not important.'

'Even if he thinks it's his fault, does that matter? Even if he drowns himself in remorse, does it change anything for that mother?'

'No,' said Jake.

'It was the car's fault, if anything. Apparently those little cars are notorious for having the pedals too close together. I think they should take them off the market. If you wanted to be really cruel, you could say it was the mother's fault, for not checking – but she was in a rush, she didn't check, it was a new car, she wasn't used to driving it and the pedals were placed very close together. That's why the accident happened, not because of you.'

'But . . .' said Jake.

'And, Jake,' Mrs Kennedy went on, ignoring him, 'a young girl has lost her little sister. She has a friend whom she would like to see, because she thinks that friend might be able to be of some comfort to her. Who is more important here, Jake, the young girl or the friend?'

'The young girl,' Jake said, still whispering. But Mrs Kennedy didn't know what Stella had said to him the last time they'd met. Nobody knew about that, except him and Stella. She didn't like him any more, and because of that, he hadn't been around lately, and because of that, Joanne had been extra excited to see him, and because of that . . .

'You might as well say it was the *baby's* fault, Jake,' said Mrs Kennedy, 'for being there.'

'That's not fair!' said Jake. Something was sitting heavily on the back of his neck, between his shoulders.

'Exactly. And it's not fair to blame yourself either.'

'But . . .' Jake started again.

Mrs Kennedy held her hand up, palm outward. She said nothing, but she shook her head.

'Goodbye, Jake,' she said, after a moment.

And she shuffle-stomped, shuffle-stomped across Jake's living-room carpet to the door.

She turned then and said, with a hint of a smile, 'Life is not a bowl of cherries, Jake, as we know. But a bowl of cherries is still a bowl of cherries.'

Jake had no idea what that meant.

He sat there, listening to her shuffle-stomping through the hall, and then the door closed, and he could see her wobbling down the garden path, and still he sat with the fish card in his hand.

39

As the car that had been waiting for Mrs Kennedy drove off, Jake's mother put her head around the living-room door. Jake still sat completely immobile.

She came in and sat beside him.

'Who exactly is that old lady?' she asked. 'She is the one who sent the card before, isn't she?'

'Yes. She's Stella's next-door neighbour's mother. She's a friend of ours. Her name is Mrs Kennedy. She likes fish paintings.'

'I see,' his mother said. 'She seems nice. But she didn't eat any Swiss roll, and neither did you.'

'Oh, I forgot,' said Jake. 'She's not supposed to eat cake. But she does, sometimes.'

'I see,' said his mother. 'Listen, Jake,' she went on. 'You know the poem about Daisy?'

'"The Daisy follows soft the Sun",' said Jake in a listless voice.

'Yes,' said his mother. 'I want to tell you the rest of the verse. Listen: "The Daisy follows soft the Sun – / And when his golden walk is done – /

Sits shyly at his feet." You know that bit, now listen to the rest: "He" (that's the Sun, Jake), "He – waking – finds the flower there – / Wherefore – Marauder – art thou here? / Because, Sir, love is sweet!"'

Jake looked at her uncomprehendingly. Everyone was speaking in riddles, and his head was too addled to decode them. The thing sitting on the back of his neck was still there. It had knotted all the muscles across his shoulders.

'The marauder is the daisy,' his mother explained. 'Isn't that an interesting word to choose? The sun is talking to the daisy, asking her why she is there, and she says, "Because, Sir, love is sweet!"'

'I don't see . . .' said Jake.

'No,' said his mother. 'But you might later. Just remember it. "Wherefore – Marauder – art thou here?"'

Jake looked at her blankly.

'Well?' she said.

'"Because, love . . . something . . ."'

'Yes,' said his mother. '"Because, Sir, love is sweet!"'

Jake stared at her. He wished his mother were an air hostess or a weather forecaster or a super-market checkout person or an engineer – anything but a poet. Poets are daft, he thought. Maybe Stella should be a lexithingy after all.

'Now, help me to bring those tea dishes into the

kitchen, and we'll make some lunch,' she said. 'I know a small marauder who is longing to see you.'

'I can't eat,' Jake said miserably.

'You will,' his mother said. 'You need to.'

40

Daisy wasn't the least bit pleased to see Jake. She started to whimper as soon as he came into the kitchen.

'There!' said Jake. 'See?'

'I don't see anything,' said his mother, 'except that Daisy's a bit fractious.'

'She doesn't like me any more,' said Jake.

'Will you stop feeling so *sorry* for yourself, Jake?' snapped his mother. 'Go and talk to your father while I get the lunch ready. He's in the garden. Weeding, I think. No, first have a glass of milk or you'll keel over.'

'He's not my father,' said Jake.

'He's the best father you've got, Jake,' said his mother stiffly, and she poured the milk for him.

'Yeah,' said Jake. 'Can we have tomato sandwiches for lunch?'

She nodded and Jake drank the milk, while she stood and watched, and then he went out into the garden. His dad was kneeling by a flower bed, not weeding, just thinking.

'Hi,' said Jake morosely. 'I'm supposed to keep out of the way till lunch. Then I'm supposed to eat lunch.'

'Wow, that's tough, Jake,' said his dad. 'Does this mean the hunger strike is over? Were your demands met?'

Jake couldn't raise a smile, but he hunkered down beside his dad.

'No,' he said. 'I wanted everyone to ignore me, but they wouldn't. I thought if I ignored them, they'd ignore me.'

'It doesn't work like that,' said his dad, starting to weed now he had some supervision. 'Here, are you up to a bit of weeding, Jake? I could do with a hand.'

Jake started to pull at a scrawny-looking weed. It resisted at first, but then he pulled nearer to the ground, a sharp tug, and the root came out of the dry earth with a satisfying squeak.

'The best way to be ignored,' his dad continued, 'is to get on with your life exactly as always. It's when you crawl into bed and face the wall that people start to take notice.'

'It's funny, that, isn't it, Dad?'

'Um,' said his dad. 'Yeah. Funny.'

'That's groundsel,' Jake said after a while, pointing to a yellow-flowered weed.

'Is it?' said his dad. 'Horrible yoke.'

They went on weeding. Jake shifted along the garden path a little in one direction and his father shifted along in the opposite direction, but they were still within chatting distance.

'I hope she doesn't put any lettuce in the tomato sandwiches,' Jake said. 'That's what we're having for lunch. I like them soggy.'

They weeded a bit more.

Then Jake's dad said, 'Jake . . .'

'I don't want to talk about it,' Jake said.

'I wasn't going to talk about it.'

'Oh?' said Jake. 'Sorry. What, then?'

'You know how we haven't been able to have a holiday this year?' his dad said. 'Because of Daisy.'

'Oh, is that why?' said Jake.

'Well, yes, we don't want to be carting a small baby around airports and train stations, do we? With prams and nappies and all the gear.'

'No,' said Jake. 'We don't.'

'And, of course, if Daisy stays at home, your mother has to stay at home too.'

'I suppose,' said Jake. 'The milk supply.'

'But, hey, Jake, that leaves us men free, doesn't it?'

'How?' asked Jake suspiciously. He'd never thought of himself as part of 'us men' before. He thought it sounded a bit pally. He could sense another fish tank coming on.

'Well, we could go off on our own, couldn't we?'

'You mean, like, camping? Fishing? Sort of father–son stuff?'

'Well, no,' said Jake's dad. 'I thought more like Old Trafford.'

'*What!*'

'You know, it's a football stadium, in . . .'

'I know what it is! Do you mean . . . oh, *Dad!*'

'Well,' said Jake's dad, 'I got a couple of tickets for the opening game of the season, and I thought maybe you'd . . . you know . . . What do you think, Jake?'

'I think . . .' Jake hesitated. 'Why are you being so nice to me? Is this because of . . .'

'Jake, are you never happy?'

'No,' said Jake.

'So you don't want to come?'

'I *do* want to come. Thanks, Dad. Oh, *yes!*' Jake punched the air.

'You're welcome.'

'Dad?'

'Hmm?'

'Do they have any art galleries over there?' asked Jake. 'With seventeenth- and eighteenth-century paintings in them?'

'You're pulling my leg, Jake.' Dad sat back on his heels and stared at Jake. His eyebrows had practically climbed up on to the top of his head.

'No, I'm not. That's when they painted fish paintings. I need to look at some of those.'

'How do you know when they painted fish paintings?' Dad asked.

'Mrs Kennedy told me. And then I looked it up, and she was right. I knew she would be.' He hadn't had to look very far. The dates had been right there, on the backs of the postcards.

'Mrs Kennedy is the old lady who was here just now?'

'Yes,' said Jake, and he went back to his weeding. 'She's got arthritis.'

'Why did she come, Jake?'

'She wants me to go to the funeral.'

'And you said . . .?' his dad asked.

'Nothing,' said Jake. 'I didn't say yes and I didn't say no.'

'Hmm,' said his dad. 'Can you not make up your mind?'

'No,' said Jake.

'Is it too sad for you?'

'No,' said Jake.

'So tell me, Jake,' Dad said. He sat back on his heels again and put on a listening face.

Jake couldn't look at him. He went on weeding, ferociously.

'You said we wouldn't talk about it,' he muttered.

'Oh yeah,' said his dad. 'I forgot.'

'We had a row,' Jake said suddenly. '*She* said, Stella, I mean, that I didn't like all her sisters and

169

I wished she didn't have so many . . . and now there's one less, so she'll think I'm glad.' A tear plopped on to the back of his hand. He stared at it. He hadn't felt it creeping down his face.

'Oh my,' said his dad. 'Oh, Jake, I see what you mean.'

Jake felt as if the thing on the back of his neck had got a little bit lighter. He wriggled his shoulders.

'But it's not true, you know,' his dad went on. 'She won't think that. She'll have forgotten all about that silly row.'

'You can't know that.'

'I just think it won't seem so important now, that's all,' his dad said. 'So much has happened that's much more important.'

'And I'm not important,' Jake said softly.

'You might just be very important,' his dad said. 'Only not in the way you think.'

'I don't know what *to do*,' wailed Jake.

'Well, think about something else for a while,' his dad suggested. 'That's what I always do when there's a hard thing to worry about, and then when you go back to thinking about the hard thing, sometimes it seems clearer.'

'OK,' said Jake.

There was silence for a few minutes, while Jake tried to think about something else.

'So *are* there any art galleries over there?' he asked after a while.

'I dunno,' Jake's dad said. 'I'm sure there must be.'

'Can we go?' Jake asked.

'Yes, if you want to, but there's an art gallery in Dublin too.'

'Is there?' said Jake. 'I didn't know. With fish paintings?'

'I dunno,' his dad said again. 'We could check, couldn't we?'

'We could,' said Jake.

There was a bit more silence. Jake thought very hard about other things.

'Jake?' said his dad after a while. 'I know you don't want to talk about it, but I think you can walk the walk. Have you ever heard that expression?'

'No,' said Jake.

'Well then, you wouldn't understand it, I suppose. Sorry I mentioned it.'

'That's OK,' said Jake.

'I only like them with pepper on them,' said his dad after a while. 'Tomato sandwiches. Do you think she'll remember to put pepper on them? It's not the same if you have to open them up and put it on afterwards. I don't know why.'

'Ah, yeah,' said Jake. 'She will. She's an ace cook.'

41

Jake sat beside Stella at the funeral, because that's where Mrs Kennedy had indicated he should sit. He'd met her at the church door and she had caught him firmly by the wrist and marched him – shuffle, stomp, shuffle, stomp – up the aisle till they got to the top, where the family sat, and she'd pointed to an empty space, a long expanse of dark brown pew beside Stella, and nudged him into the seat. He'd slid along on his bottom till he was sitting next to her.

Stella looked like a ghost, her skin even paler than usual, her hair all loose about her thin shoulders, like a ghost girl's, and she was wearing the kind of dress she never wore, in pale lemon with long sleeves and buttons all up the front and a turndown collar. She seemed like a character in an old movie. She reminded Jake of the portrait of the beautiful girl that hung on the stairwell in Mr Kennedy's house. She didn't look like the girl, but she had the same expression on her face.

The other children sat in a row in the seat behind, with their parents. They sat unnaturally still, and all their hair was brushed, so that they looked like paintings too, paintings of themselves. There was a scent of lilies in the air. Nothing seemed natural, and everything was too calm. There was organ music.

Nobody explained why Stella needed a whole pew to herself, but then one or two people came and sat at the other end of it. They sat quietly and riffled through notebooks and prayerbooks and looked grave and important.

They said nothing to each other, Jake and Stella. They didn't even look at each other. Jake thought he would burst if he caught Stella's eye, and he imagined she probably felt the same about him, and neither of them wanted to burst and spoil everything.

He wondered if he should say he was sorry, about . . . whatever it was. Though he wasn't. He was sorry about Joanne, but he couldn't be sorry about the other thing, because he didn't understand what he was supposed to have done. He wouldn't mind *saying* he was sorry, though, if it would help. He wouldn't mind doing anything if it would help. He felt as if his head was going to split right down the middle like a cracked-open walnut from the sheer pressure of how sorry he felt about Joanne and how sorry he felt for Stella and for her family.

Sorrow was like a taut wire in his brain, and if he moved, he felt, it would slice right through and cleave his brain in two, the way the cheese-cutter did in the supermarket – it sliced right through the cheese, even though it was only a piece of wire, but it was held very taut, and that was what made it so powerful.

It became clear later why Stella was in that special pew. It was for the people doing the readings and saying the prayers, so they could slip out easily and go to the top of the church when their turn came.

When it was her turn to go to the top, Stella read, in a high, restrained voice, like a person reading the news, from Joanne's favourite book, *One Fish Two Fish Red Fish Blue Fish*, and Jake's heart broke all over again. He could hear the little voice in his head, 'One fiss, two fiss, wed fiss, boo fiss,' but Stella didn't cry, and Jake didn't either, though his head ached with the effort.

Even if it was my fault, he said to himself – which it wasn't – it's not my fault that it was my fault. It was a complicated thought, but it seemed to have its own comforting logic. He felt as if the cheese-cutter in his head had slackened a little bit. He thought maybe his head wouldn't burst now.

When Stella came back to her seat, Jake did dare to catch her eye, and he mouthed, 'Well done.'

She looked away.

Just for a moment, Jake felt offended. Then he remembered who the important one was and he stopped feeling sorry for himself.

Later, when Jake was just getting into his dad's car to go home and Stella was standing with a group of her cousins from the country, she waved to him. That was all. But it made him feel better.

On the way home, he tried to think of things that might make Stella feel better. But he couldn't think of a single one. That made him feel worse.

It would probably go on like that for ages, he thought. Feeling better and then feeling worse. Only for Stella and the rest, there'd be more feeling worse and not much feeling better.

42

The summer felt old. After the funeral came the football and fish paintings trip, and after that there was nothing to look forward to except school. To distract them from that terrible thought, Stella's dad had suggested that they should build a tree house in the cherry tree. So that is what they were doing, building the tree house, and he was helping them.

The official line was that *they* were helping *him*, but it was pretty clear to Stella and Jake that he didn't know the first thing about the requirements for a good tree house for the use of five children and their friends. But Jake had found a recipe, as he called it, for a tree house, in a library book. It looked unnecessarily complicated, but they could adapt it. They didn't need a veranda, he reasoned, or an attic. And you could always put on an extension later, he and Stella had agreed, if necessary. Anyway, they didn't want to fill up the whole tree. They had to leave room for the cherries next year.

They were only at the stage of measuring up and planning. They hadn't got as far as buying the wood yet, much less actually sawing and hammering. Stella's dad said he'd do that part, and Stella wanted it finished quickly, so the children could play in it for at least a month before the weather started to get chilly and the evenings short.

'We're all going to be Cotter Burkes,' Jake told Stella. He watched her spreading her arms across to see how wide the thing was going to be. 'Did I tell you?'

'I thought you said you were going to be a fish painter,' she said. 'I can't keep up with you. Now you want to be a cotterberk, whatever that is. Hold your end of the tape steady, Dad, the measurements will be out if you let it bend like that!'

Jake snorted a small laugh. 'It's not a job, it's a name. My mum's a Cotter. So am I. That's our surname. Dad's a Burke. But now that we're all an official family, since they got married and every-thing, we thought we'd join up the names so everyone could be the same. It was my idea.'

'We're just Dalys,' Stella said. 'But we don't mind being friends with double-barrelled people, do we, Daddy? Will you have to change your passport, Jake?'

'I haven't got a passport. I've never been abroad. Except to Old Trafford, but you don't need a pass-port for England.'

'You should get one,' said Stella's dad, sticking a pencil purposefully behind his ear. 'In case you need to run away from home. All my children have them expressly for that purpose, or so they tell me.'

'I don't think I will want to run away. Or not that far.'

'When I met you first,' Stella said, '– remember, in the supermarket? – you were a proper little bundle of misery. You looked then as if you wanted to run away, as far away as you could get.'

'Was I? Did I? I don't remember.'

'Oh, yes. You didn't like babies. And you didn't like girls. You especially didn't like *me*. Don't say a word, I know you didn't. I wanted you to be my friend because I thought you looked more interesting than most boys, but I had to work very hard at it. I had to *follow you home* to see where you lived. I don't think you liked your dad too well either. You only liked fish and football. You didn't even seem to like yourself very much.'

'I do like my dad.'

'You didn't like him much then. I don't understand why. Just because he isn't the one who ran away is not a very good reason.'

'Well, he laughed at me.'

'Everyone laughs at you, Jake. That's nothing to get upset about. You can make a career out of that, you know. It's called being a comedian.'

'But I want to be a fish painter,' Jake pointed out. 'Or something along those lines.'

'Ah, yes,' said Brian. 'I remember. The boy with the fish tank, that was you. Remember the day you took the girls over there, Stella, and Joey came running home all excited about the "fiss".'

Jake froze. He didn't know where to look. They'd mentioned the thing he didn't dare even to think about.

Stella was laughing too. How could they *laugh*? After the dreadful thing that had happened. He couldn't understand that, how they weren't all swimming in a black murk of depression all the time. He thought about Daisy, and he shivered at the thought of anything happening to her, anything like the horrible thing that had happened to Joanne; the thing that had nearly happened to Nuala Something.

'How come you can laugh?' he asked.

There was silence for a few moments. Perhaps he shouldn't have asked.

Jake sucked in his breath and waited, and then Stella said, 'Because we can't always be crying. That's why. And anyway it would be silly only to cry, when you can laugh sometimes.'

'That's it,' her dad said. 'There arc enough sad things to cry about without crying about the funny things too.'

'I see,' said Jake. Something clicked in his head.

Something he hadn't understood before. 'Like how life is not a bowl of cherries, but a bowl of cherries is still a bowl of cherries.'

Stella stared at him. She didn't get it. But her dad did.

'Something like that,' he said. 'Sort of.'

'Mrs Kennedy told me that,' Jake explained to Stella.

'Oh,' said Stella, but she still didn't see.

It didn't matter.

'Let's go to the park,' Jake said, 'while your dad is getting the wood and stuff. Let's have a game of one-a-side football, you know, goal to goal, and afterwards, I'll buy you an ice cream. I got extra pocket money this week for cleaning the downstairs windows.'

'OK,' said Stella. 'Sounds good. Let's go. If that's OK with you, Dad? Can you manage the rest by yourself?'

'That's OK,' said Brian, who had taken the pencil from behind his ear and was writing down measurements. 'I think I can cope. Just about.'

'And then,' said Jake, 'after the ice creams, we can go to see Mrs Kennedy. I want to tell her about the tree house. I bet she'd love to hear about it.'

'Yeah,' said Stella, 'and we have to make sure she doesn't let her son put in an objection with An Bord Pleanála.'

'An Bord *what*?' said Jake.

'The planning people,' Stella explained. '*You* know. They stop you building things.'

'Oh yeah,' said Jake. 'Daisy-murderer,' he hissed. 'Fish-faker.'

'Curmudgeon,' added Stella. 'That's my word of the week. Good, isn't it? And after all that, can we go and see Daisy?'

'Yeah,' said Jake. 'The small marauder.'

'What?'

'Oh . . . nothing. Come *on*, then. Let's go!'